D0629089

The Dirty Shame Hotel

The Dirty Shame Hotel

and other stories

RON BLOCK

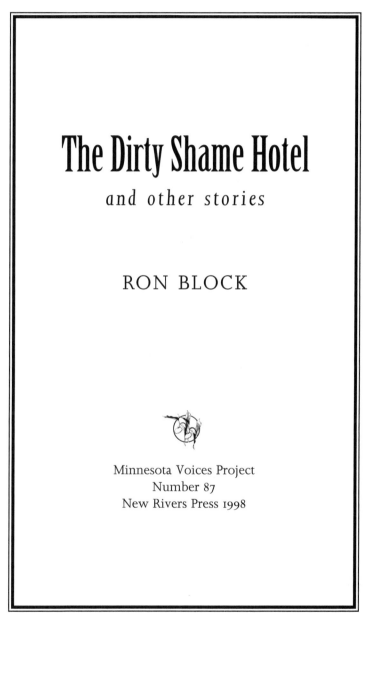

Minnesota Voices Project
Number 87
New Rivers Press 1998

© 1998 by Ron Block. All rights reserved
First Edition
Printed in the United States of America
Library of Congress Catalog Card Number: 97-69843
ISBN: 0-89823-187-6
Edited by C. W. Truesdale
Copyedited by Anne Running
Cover painting, "First Fruits of Solitude," by Tom Bartek, acrylic on
    linen canvas, 48½" x 40½", 1989
Book design and typesetting by Steven Canine

New Rivers Press is a nonprofit literary press dedicated to publishing
the very best emerging writers in our region, nation, and world.

The publication of The Dirty Shame Hotel has been made possible
by generous grants from the Jerome Foundation; the Minnesota State Arts
Board (through an appropriation by the Minnesota Legislature); the
North Dakota Council on the Arts; Target Stores, Dayton's, and Mervyn's
by the Dayton Hudson Foundation; and the James R. Thorpe Foundation.

Additional support has been provided by the Elmer L. and Eleanor J.
Andersen Foundation, the Beim Foundation, the General Mills Foundation,
Liberty State Bank, the McKnight Foundation, the Star Tribune / Cowles
Media Company, and the contributing members of New Rivers Press.

New Rivers Press
420 North Fifth Street, Suite 910
Minneapolis, MN 55401

www.mtn.org/newrivpr

The best of these stories are dedicated
to
Joe and Jean

Contents

Acknowledgments

I gratefully acknowledge the publications in which the following stories previously appeared: "Zadoc Xenophone Cannot See Bright New Moons. Can Vera Montague?" *Short Story*, vol. 2, no. 1 (1994); and "Land of the Midnight Blonde," *Tamaqua*, vol. 6, no. 2. (Winter 1997).

Zadoc Xenophon Cannot View Bright New Moons. Can Vera Montague?

THE TYPEWRITER ALONE must have weighed all of thirty pounds—an enormous, brand-new Underwood Standard, No. 5, along with an up-to-date instruction manual and a ream of paper. But Vera lugged it by hand the two miles back to the farm, and by the time she got there, she could not flex her arms without them springing back. Somehow this sensation made her feel like she was already part of a machine.

Ignoring the stares of her sister—and thankful that her brother-in-law Henry was not in the house—Vera carried the machine through the parlor and set it up on the vanity in her bedroom. The manual was designed with the spine at the top of the page; that way it could stand up on its own beside the typewriter, each page to be flipped over the top to the next. After trimming the wick and lighting the lamp, Vera got right to work:

The Typist
by Dr. J. E. Fuller
A Course of Lessons in the Proper Fingering
and the Efficient Manipulation of the Typewriter
Copyright, 1918, by the Phonographic Institute Company

After reading the preface, wherein Dr. Fuller made a case for "self-reliance and self–actualization arising from the concentration and power of will to be derived from the art of typing," Vera turned to the diagrams explaining the dense anatomy of the machine: the platen locking piece, the platen knobs, the paper table, the tabulator rack and stop, the platen scale. She memorized these, and then she started to study the fifty-three keys that, excluding capitals, produced eighty-four characters, only pausing to ask herself—

Why weren't they in alphabetical order? They didn't seem to have any particular order at all—unless they were ordered for their efficiency and rapidity of use. But then why would her handiest finger, her index finger on her right hand, be positioned over the letter J? Why wouldn't this finger be positioned over a vowel, say E or A, or at least over the letter S, which was obviously more common than J? The arrangement made no sense to her.

Maybe when she learned this art, she would slowly understand this deeper, more mysterious arrangement of the alphabet, a mystery she could sense right off in the way the small L doubled for the number one: some hidden connection between letters and numbers, a hint of a mysterious transformation to come.

She continued to read the text, discovering that the exclamation point was seldom used in business correspondence. That seemed sad to her, because almost every day she longed to be startled by something new. Would nothing in business merit exclamation?

Briefly leaving off her enterprise, she looked out her window at a large elm tree with nighttime creeping up into its branches. Her brother Charlie had planted that tree. Her brother had always said that someday he would break into the branches and discover enough furniture there to fill a house—but instead he had moved to California, while the tree stayed behind.

Tonight, Vera could see the tree reaching out in an attempt to restrain the moon in the webbing of its branches, but otherwise there was nothing in the frame of Vera's window but the flattened Plains, which lost their depth in the twilight. The Plains, she thought, deserved their name. They promised nothing, and they always kept their promises.

Returning to her lesson, Vera was delighted to find that she could produce the exclamation point, "for the rare conditions of its highly discouraged use," by striking an apostrophe and then backing up and striking a period, another mysterious symbol, another doubling and transformation. She decided to celebrate this discovery by typing her name: Capital V. The carriage jumped up, thumped down, small e, little r, a, space. Capital H. The shift keys were the hardest to push. She had to use her little fingers to push them—o-l-q-u-i-s-t—and then she put on an exclamation point as a finishing touch: Vera Holquist!

It was the first time she'd ever seen her name in print, and she studied it, feeling a dull sense of dread that she could not understand. A spoken name somehow seemed to add someone to the world. You could call out to someone and make that person come to you. But a printed name could very possibly take someone away. She remembered the cleanly printed name on her mother's tombstone. In this manner, she discovered that the machine possessed a terrible power, and she knew she would have to be circumspect in using it.

❀   ❀   ❀

When Vera waddled in through the door with the strange machine, her sister Holly was in the kitchen, bending over a tin tub to wash the twins, while her older daughter, the lonely one, stood to one side and brooded. Without saying a word, Vera lugged the typewriter through the kitchen and on back toward her bedroom, setting it on her vanity, right in front of the mirror.

Holly let an hour go by while she tried to handle the slippery babies, attempting to get them dressed, and fed, and settled in for the night. All this time she could hear Vera in the bedroom, making a sound like the snapping of beans, only louder. Holly didn't have much of a temper to begin with, so it took quite a while for her temper to build. But finally she stepped into the bedroom and said, "Vera! Vera, look at me! What *are you doing?*" Vera had just finished several lines of typing—

Vera Holquist! Vera Holquist! Vera Holquist! Vera Holquist!
Vera Holquist! Vera Holquist! Vera Holquist! Vera Holquist!

and she blushed. Hardly able to restrain herself, Holly reminded Vera that she had been home all day, washing clothes, cooking, cleaning, minding the children, "and," she said, "I'd *hoped* to get part of the garden in, but never mind *me.* I'll be fine. Don't bother to tell me that you've just decided to wander off and busy yourself with a lot of nonsense and saddle me with all the work with the children, not to mention Henry's—"

"Is he back from the field?" Vera asked, suddenly nervous.

Holly was astounded. For Vera not to notice this, in a house so small, was quite the confession. Even for Vera, such absentmindedness was completely out of the ordinary, so now Holly became concerned. "Are you feeling well?"

"Oh, yes," Vera said. "I think so. It's just that—"

Vera turned to the machine and gestured, seeming to indicate that her lapse was somehow the machine's fault, and Holly took in the sight. She nodded. She had grown used to new machines and the disruptions they caused. Her husband Henry was among the first to acquire the angry farm machinery that wrecked the silence of the Plains, and Holly's general response to these gadgets was not so much to object, but to grow more quiet, as if there were only so much noise allotted to the Plains, and Henry's machines had taken hers.

Folks throughout the county generally thought that Holly was a sweet woman, a godly woman. Holly enjoyed the burden of being long-suffering, which was a fundamental quality of righteousness. On the other hand, folks thought that Vera expected too much, and so it was said that she would have nothing, as if her life were a Bible parable.

"Vera? What is this thing? You're starting to give me fits!"

Vera bowed her head and didn't say anything. Her day had been so improbable that she didn't know how to explain it.

"Speak to me! Where did you get this thing? Where have you been all day? And what kind of nonsense are you up to now?"

❀　❀　❀

That day, Vera had been taking one of her many walks, daydreaming, when she noticed that men were erecting crosses along the road. The sight put her in mind of the Biblical road that traveled to Golgotha, a chilling sight, but Vera's curiosity outran her fear. She went up to the men and asked them what they were doing, and that's how she found that a telephone company was weaving the country together. The telephone company even had an office in town.

Without really understanding why, without a plan, she walked several miles to this office, and there a group of men were standing around in alpaca jackets and vests, with hands gripping their lapels as if they were posing for a photograph that History planned to take of them. They were watching and advising another group of men, workers, who were stuffing a cabinet full of black rubber veins.

Finally the men noticed her, so Vera introduced herself. As if they were doing only what was expected of them, the men started to explain the activity they were engaged in. Telephone, they said, meant distant sound. Doctors could be summoned from miles away. You would be able to talk to a friend without traveling there and back. A new age. The wide world would suddenly compress and be more of an intimate place. Our voices alone would do our work, like ghosts, without the assistance of our bodies. When the men told her this, they seemed to be performing for her, practicing their oratory or reciting from a holy text espousing a new religion.

"So is there anything else we can do for you, young lady?"

Without considering it beforehand, she said that she was looking for a job.

❀　❀　❀

"A job?" Holly said. "Doesn't Henry give us both enough to do?"

One of the children started to cry, so Holly hurried out of the room, looking back at her sister with almost a frightened look. Feeling guilty, Vera followed, but a sudden image of Charlie came into her mind, so she stood there and daydreamed about him for a moment.

Charlie was a large man, and most of the household tasks he tried to perform didn't seem to fit his proportions. Once he tried to thread a needle, but the sight seemed so ridiculous to Holly and Vera that they couldn't help but laugh at him.

And then there was the time that Charlie tried to write a letter. He hunkered over the kitchen table, gripping a small pencil in his large farmer's hands. His fingers were so swollen from work that they looked like stumps, and he concentrated so intently that the tip of his tongue peeked out from between his teeth. The force with which he scrawled the words made it seem like he was carving something in wood.

He had been composing a letter to a friend in California, someone he'd met in the train station. The man introduced himself as Gamble. He was only passing through and seemed amused that anyone lived in the empty place where they had made their home. He kidded Charlie about this, and Charlie enjoyed being kidded, and so this man obliged. They quickly became friends. Charlie even convinced him to put off the rest of his journey and come back to the farm.

At first Henry was suspicious about this visitor, but Gamble seemed to think that farmwork was a great adventure, and he was willing to do it for the wages of a sunrise, three meals, and a game of rummy in the evening. A few weeks later, he boarded the train and continued his trip, and it was then that Vera noticed that Charlie seemed to be angry with her. Normally talkative, Charlie brooded in silence. When she asked Charlie what was wrong he snapped at her. "What's the matter with you, anyhow?"

Vera felt herself shrink.

"I mean, didn't you see how Gamble stood up every time you walked into the room? Didn't you even notice how he'd smile at you? Do you want to be a lonely old woman? I mean, if you'd just given him a little attention, just the littlest bit, why, he might have stayed!"

"You wanted him to stay?" Vera asked.

"Of course I did!"

Vera didn't know what to say to that. She still didn't. Usually Charlie was her champion and her defender, and she hated the fact that her strongest memory of him was one where he was completely out of character.

As she stood in the hall listening to Holly trying to quiet the twins, the good memory went from bad to worse. A month later Charlie got a letter from Gamble, all the way from California. Charlie walked around with the letter in his pocket. He studied it for several days. She noticed that Charlie would read the letter to himself at least once each evening. She watched as he struggled to carve a reply with a pencil stub.

This, too, went on for several nights before Charlie gave up and announced to them all that since he couldn't write a reply, he was just going to have to go to California himself. His friend Gamble had said that there were whole forests in California, and they didn't have to plant them. Gamble said that the land didn't just run on forever there. It had an edge. Gamble said it was called a shore. He said it was something to rest your eyes on so you didn't go crazy.

So Charlie boarded the train and didn't come back.

Vera mourned for him. Having lost her father, her mother, and now her brother, she was afraid now of losing Holly and Henry, and so for months afterward, she couldn't bear to be alone. She discovered that there was comfort in crowds in a land so empty, so she taught herself to see the crowds wherever they might appear. The pond crowded up with clouds. The town crowded up with names. But even so, when she and Holly and the children stepped outside the house, she sometimes felt there was too much air between them. A sudden wind, and she'd lose them forever.

Vera remembered all this in the blank daze of loneliness. She had lost her brother, she thought, because she couldn't be the sister that he wanted her to be, and now she was going to lose her sister for the same reason. Her anxiety growing, all she could think of to do was to go back to her typing, hoping that would calm her, and there she discovered that a page was still in the carriage, marked in the middle of the page by the single letter X. Vera looked at the page and suddenly whole sentences started to run though her mind, so complete and clear that they seemed to be spoken by someone else. Or perhaps it was something she read in the typing manual.

"Alone, the letter X means absolutely nothing. When covering another letter, it means mistake, Xed out, this doesn't matter. But alone, it means nothing. And even at that, it has very few letters that will even keep its company. Excuse. Except. Exaggeration. Box."

Again, she looked at the X. She didn't remember typing it.

⁂   ⁂   ⁂

Success in typing depends upon the following essentials. Sit erect, near enough to the machine that the ARMS may hang naturally beside the body. The relative height of CHAIR and DESK should be such to bring the ELBOWS about an inch lower than the TOP of the DESK. This will give the FOREARMS an upward slant. The HANDS should be kept CLOSE TO THE KEYS, the palms parallel with the slope of the keyboard; but the WRISTS should not be permitted to droop so that the palms touch the frame of the machine. The FINGERS should be WELL CURVED—POINTED DOWNWARD. Eyes must be kept on the book. Each finger must be kept within its own division. Strike the keys with a SNAPPY BLOW. Write at an EVEN, STEADY rate of speed—not irregularly or jerkily. . . .

After an hour of practicing this position, Vera's whole body began to cramp, so she went out into the kitchen to help her sister get the table ready, recalling that, before their mother had died, she had advised the two girls with the following:

"When you get married, even if you do not have supper ready, ALWAYS have the TABLE SET when your husband comes in from work. That way he will NOT complain. In the middle of the afternoon, change your dress. That way, when your husband comes in, he will notice that you LOOK DIFFERENT, although you should not expect him to say HOW. But that way he will think that you've gotten a lot done. Always CLEAN THE SURFACES of counters first. Clean what he will see first, first. Do the corners only if you have time. If you are very far behind in making supper, FRY SOME ONIONS, even if you do not plan to serve them. If he smells something cooking, he will NOT complain."

❀   ❀   ❀

Henry came in, looking tired. The table was set. Onions were frying. He looked around the room once, wandered to the sink, washed, wandered into the other room, and started to nap. After an hour, they woke him so that he could eat. He ate. Then they went into the parlor where Vera read to them from *Pilgrim's Progress*, about which Henry would make his customary derisive comments.

Henry was a godless man, and he gloried in this, using this fact to his great advantage in his dealing with the other farmers. They took his godlessness as a sign that he was fearless—and they despaired of ever getting the upper hand on him, no matter that God would be on their side.

Once, Vera heard Henry laugh at a farmer who proclaimed that this land was God's country. Henry said, "Oh yes, God's country, sure! There ain't no *God*, and there ain't *nothing here*, if that's what you mean!"

The farmer grew dark and furious, but after that he shied away from Henry. Even when Henry sought to acquire the farmer's land, the farmer made a short deal of it and accepted Henry's initial bid.

Henry farmed the land because he was angry at it. He made a good businessman and drove hard bargains and made his family money because he was angry at the other farmers. He worked himself to exhaustion. Even while Vera was taking her walk that day, she could see

Henry hunched over the wheel of the tractor, as if he were forcing it forward himself, concentrating while he tore an edge into the otherwise seamless world.

Tonight, during the reading of *Pilgrim's Progress*, Henry laughed especially hard at the appearance in the allegory of a Mr. Legality, who offered the traveler, Christian, a comfortable way to remove the burdens of his sin.

"Oh, I've heard it all," he said, disgusted. "First Christian abandons his family, goes tearing off through swamps looking for some kind of city in the stars, just because he had a bad dream, and now he's ignoring good legal advice. Well, I tell you, the Christian farmers around here don't take a dim view toward lawyers." Henry chuckled a bit more, and then lapsed into a yawn. "Well, enough of this nonsense. I'm going to bed."

Holly waited for her husband to get out of earshot, and then she narrowed her eyes at her sister and said, "Well, I want to thank you for being so prompt in helping me with supper."

"You're welcome," Vera said.

"Don't expect *me* to explain to him what you're up to. You'll have to explain it yourself, and please, Vera, do it soon, so he doesn't blame *me* when things are not getting done."

"I'll tell him. I'll tell him tomorrow."

"I can tell you right now that he won't like it. He'll think that you are trying to shame him with this nonsense."

After Holly trudged off to bed, Vera sat up for a while, thinking.

What did her sister mean by "nonsense"? That was maybe the third or fourth time Holly had used it that day alone, and it didn't even seem like the kind of word that she normally used. Henry, yes—but not Holly. It seemed like an odd word, a stuffy word, a tight box. Holly used to get into these silly moods where she and Vera could laugh at everything. What had happened to all that?

Trying to relax, Vera stepped out on the porch for a spell, breathing in the night. She was glad to see that the moon had finally made its way out of Charlie's tree. From here on out, it had clear sailing across the sky. It was a full moon, a big, infectious yawn of a moon. Vera yawned back at it, then went back in the house and into her bedroom, where the typewriter hunkered on her vanity, seeming to be waiting for her.

At first, Vera tried to ignore the typewriter. She put on her nightgown and climbed into bed. She tried to put herself to sleep by retracing Christian's travels, but this was useless. In the moonlight, the machine was like a small animal that needed to be petted, so she went to it. She sat down at the vanity, looked at her own image in the mirror, where it was surrounded by fleurs-de-lis and curlicues that seemed to nag at her about her own vanity, and then put three sheets of paper into the carriage to soften the sound. After studying the position of the keys again, Vera started her next lesson:

LESSON TWO: THE HOME KEYS
all ask sad; ask all sad; sad all ask; all sad ask;
all ask dad; sad lass asks; sad lad asks; all fall;

and then—

alas alfalfa falls; alas alfalfa falls; alas; alas;

and then—

a sad lass asks; sad dad has a flask; a sad lad asks;
dad asks a flask; a glass falls; a jag; a gash; alas;
a glass flash; all fall sad; alas; a lad; a lass; alas;

She typed each of the sentences over several times. The page filled up, and her mind started to drift. No doubt Holly and Henry would look at this page and say, "Nonsense," because the sentences were. And yet there seemed to be a mysterious story at work here. Vera could feel the story in a physical way, creeping up her arms as she typed. A sad family. Drunkenness. Disaster. Grief. What a story, she thought. And then she stopped typing because she realized that this was Henry's story.

Henry's father was a minister, a farmer, and a very mean drunk. Henry also had a sister, who had reacted to her father's religion even more strongly than Henry did. She was a big, friendly woman who visited them at least twice a year. She had furs and jewelry, and even a car the last time she stopped, and Henry always turned shy whenever anyone asked about her. He said that she owned a hotel, but that story was easy enough to see through.

It was curious, but now that Vera thought of it, she realized that Henry's sister had been the first to plant in Vera's mind the idea that she, Vera, should have her own job. Henry's sister had said that a woman with her own money had the means to follow through on her wishes, and yet this was advice from an immodest woman.

Leaving the typewriter for a moment, Vera reviewed the day to see if there were a clue buried among the many moments. Without realizing what she planned to do, she had walked into the telephone office and asked them for a job. They smiled at her. Immediately she had said, "I believe I might be useful." And then they—

She tried to recall the tone of their words, their expressions. And then they *humored* her—she realized that now. But was that true? After all, they *had* interviewed her. They asked her, first off, if she was married, and when she said no, they might have looked upon her sadly. They might have even pitied her, but that *was* the answer they wanted to hear, wasn't it? And then they asked her more meaningful questions: Did she know double-entry accounting? She astonished them by saying yes. She'd learned it in high school and practiced it on Henry's accounts. They said, Henry? "My sister's husband. I live with them." The world of this answer, the troubles and conflicts, meant nothing to them. They simply proceeded to the next question: Could she type? She considered lying, but couldn't. They looked distracted. But then she surprised herself.

She said, "But what if, say in a week, I taught myself this? What if I learned to type? I believe—" Suddenly she felt embarrassed, but she said it anyway: "I believe that I can learn anything."

For a while, the men were completely quiet, as if they were shocked, mortified by her bragging. At least that's what she thought until one said, "Well, if she can learn to type in a *week*"—he smiled at the idea, as if it were nearly impossible—"well, then, maybe we should give her the job." Having said that, his smile grew broad and knowing, proclaiming his ingenuity to the other men, as if he had solved a complex problem in a clever way.

"Do you have a typewriter I could borrow?" Vera asked. And for some reason all the men laughed at once.

"A go-getter, she is."

"We'd better watch this one," said another, "or she might have *our* jobs." And they all laughed again. . . .

❀   ❀   ❀

Vera found herself back in her bedroom, pacing furiously, almost relieved by her anger. She wished that she could become this angry with her sister and Henry. She couldn't, and so she appreciated her anger as long as she could, until it became so intense that it brought tears into her eyes.

She was angry because she knew now what bothered her about the day. Those men had laughed at her, condescended to her. And she realized that even if she got this job, those men would condescend to her every day.

And *that* was one thing she did not face at home. Henry was a tyrant, yes, but he never treated her like a child. He bossed her around, but when she balanced his books, he listened and understood that she knew better than he did the flow and drift of money from the farm. He acknowledged that she was a valuable asset.

Wouldn't it be better for her to let this new plan go? To stick around the house and help her sister and balance the books? To let Henry worry about the ways of the world, and money, and jobs? Yes, she would do that. She would take the typewriter back and tell those men that she didn't want their job, that they could laugh at someone else. And yet—

And yet at that moment she was so angry that she knew she could not go to sleep. She did not feel like reading, and she had no one to talk to. All she could think of to do was to go back to her lesson, so that's what she did—"but only until I grow tired and fall asleep," she thought. "And then I'll never touch that machine again."

LESSON THREE:
THE HOME KEYS WITH THIRD ROW VOWELS AND COMMA
Here, you will progress away from the home row. Endeavor to keep your fingers curled, your wrist slightly lower than your hands. Keep a straight back. Do not look at the keys. Begin typing:

a safe idea is laid aside, a safe idea is laid aside,
a safe idea is laid aside, a safe idea is laid aside,

Repeat these phrases until you have mastered them. Only then should you go on to the next exercise, which may, at first, seem easier since it mainly involves the index finger. You will find, however, that the question mark is often the hardest key to find:

LESSON FOUR:
INDEX FINGER, VOWELS, AND QUESTION MARK
Hug tin boy? Boy tin, boy hug, tin boy. Hug tin boy?
Hag hug tin, hag hug tub, hag hug tin tub, hag hug tin?

Suddenly she thought of another plan. Perhaps she should begin writing Gamble. If, through the mail, she could succeed in making him love her, he might come back and bring Charlie with him. She thought about this plan quite a bit. If she typed well enough to be able to do that, then that would be enough. It was a worthwhile plan, and it seemed possible. She even attempted to compose her first letter at the typewriter, slowly, first finding the words in her head and then searching for the keys. She looked at her hands and slouched over the keyboard and broke every single rule that Dr. Fuller had taught her, and then, perhaps in punishment for this, she started to feel dizzy. Or perhaps it was the fumes from the kerosene lamp that caused the lightness in her head.

She tried to read her letter to Gamble, but then she suddenly decided that if she went to the trouble of writing this letter, she might as well try to get that job. And anyway, her letter to Gamble sounded silly—full of words and phrases that she found embarrassing even when she read them in romantic books.

Putting the letter aside, she got up and padded barefoot toward the kitchen, noticing how the floor of the house was starting to bow, the wood swelling in the slow motion of time. From the hand pump next to the sink, she got herself a drink of water, and then she felt better. She sipped the water slowly as she looked out the window at the tree that Charlie had planted. From this angle, the moon was back in the branches.

Charlie had always told her that he could see tables and chairs in the branches. The kitchen window rippled with imperfections and tiny air bubbles. He said to her once that each bubble in the glass was a tiny world. At night, if you looked at them from the right angle, the very impact of your vision would scatter them among the stars. That's not exactly how he said it, but that's the image she got from what he said.

Padding back to her bedroom, Vera paused briefly at the door of Henry and Holly's bedroom. She was glad to hear Henry snore. To tell Henry her plans, if they still were her plans, would be bad enough. But to wake him up and steal away his sleep, and to have him discover her in her selfishness, would be horrible.

Maybe she was taking quite a chance in working this late at night, but Henry's sleep was as deep as a winter frost. From the way folks talked in town, one might think that Henry's godless sleep would be fitful, that he would secretly fear that his unacknowledged maker would reach out and touch him, silence him, in the middle of the night. That was not true. Henry slept the self-satisfied sleep of one who has worked hard and done well.

Vera knew that Holly often felt distressed by her husband's lack of religious beliefs, but the only time Holly had fought with him that Vera remembered was when he tried to prevent her from having the girls baptized. In the end, Henry acted as if he were humoring her, and thinking of that, Vera revised her earlier opinion. Yes, Henry sometimes condescended, but only on matters of religion. The important thing was that he finally relented, dressed up in an old Sunday suit, and went with them all to the church. He smiled with indulgence throughout the ceremony. This showed that he was not so proud that he could not give in to compromise, and in itself this was a hopeful sign.

As for Holly—well, Holly seemed to get used to anything. It was a good quality. It even helped her to survive. But she adapted to changes so quickly and completely that it suggested she was weak, and all too soon these changes soon assumed the force of habits. She was that way about religion, too: her beliefs seemed to be merely habitual and not keenly felt. Henry's godlessness was more passionate, for this was his license to fight, which he dearly loved. He used his abilities to argue to strip all mystery from the world, and yet Holly's constancy, her habits, seemed to do the same.

It would not be easy to go against their will. If only Charlie were here to stand behind her.

Vera studied the keys again. They were harder to push than she had expected. She knew that tomorrow her forearms would ache, but in time they'd grow stronger. She began again. The doctor informed her:

> Now we venture into stranger land. Free yourself from the sense of what you are typing, for if you struggle to keep the sense of the words in your mind, it will only slow you down. Let the strokes of the keys be even and regular. Many have said that it is useful to imagine them as the ticking of a clock first, and then the beating of a drum. Concentrate in a relaxed and easy fashion, and let a peace flow over you that is not dissimilar to the attitude of prayer. Empty your mind of the past and future, of all struggles and turmoil, of all hopes and doubts, and begin typing:
>
>> Night hag grown artful; artful night; artful night hag; victory bright; nocturnal hag; bright nocturnal; artful hag; nocturnal victory; artful night hag; artful night. Bright nocturnal art. Bright night. Victory bright.

As Vera practiced, she found that these odd phrases repeated themselves at random, and she was surprised to see how quickly the lower edge of the page came up through the carriage, surprised to see this page was densely filled with words. What had happened to her sense of time? She could not even begin to guess how long it had taken to fill this page.

Examining her work, she was proud to see there were very few mistakes. But it was an odd set of words that this author, J. E. Fuller, had chosen. She wondered what kind of man he would be, and why he chose these words that seemed so much like a spell he was casting over her, especially as she typed them over and over.

Putting a fresh page into the typewriter, she wrote down the time and began to type this lesson again, and this time she kept her self-awareness enough to see that there was a noticeable transformation in the patterns of her thought. At first, she knew she was typing the doctor's words. She could almost hear his voice—educated, slightly stuffy, droning on a bit. Then—she couldn't say exactly when—but then the words stopped seeming like his. They seemed like her words. Words that were coming from deep within her. Words so true that she didn't have to think to type them. She just typed, but the words came so easily that it seemed as though she were speaking them.

They were like a chant, wherein one asked God for a favor, a bless-ing. They were like a spell, one she knew she could work. She could feel the spell working as she typed the phrases over and over. The spell brought strength into her fingertips as she snapped the keys. They sounded like small twigs breaking in a forest, small bones of an animal breaking as a larger one took it in its teeth. And then, briefly, before the words covered the page, they seemed like they belonged to no one.

LESSON SEVEN:
THE CULMINATION OF OUR FIRST NIGHT OF LESSONS

As our lessons continue, one will find that the benefits of typing are many. For some, the discipline of typing will blaze the path to self-determination and the fruits of gainful work. For others, the focus and practice involved will build character. One might even find that by typing the simple and complete sentences of the fol-lowing lesson, one will begin to internalize their benevolent morals. Remember to sit erect with your hands slightly curved, and begin:

A joke may very quickly fix in your mind a helpful, wise, but puzzling proverb. A joke may very quickly fix in your mind a helpful, wise, but puzzling proverb. . . .

Jim was a lazy fellow who could never remember the quaint maxim that the pillow kills more than the gun. Jim was a lazy fellow who could never remember the quaint maxim that the pillow kills more than the gun. . . .

Xadoc Xenophone cannot view bright new moons. Can Vera Montague? Zadoc Xenophone cannot view bright new moons. Can Vera Montague?

Suddenly, she stopped typing and examined the words. This was a trick, Vera thought. The first two sentences, as the doctor had promised, offered a "simple point"—but the final adage was nonsense, even more unnerving because it used her first name. She felt like throwing the type-writer. She felt angry and betrayed, and yet when she calmed herself she didn't quite know why the lesson had angered her.

Perhaps it was because she had typed the nonsense phrase with the same earnestness and attention as she had typed the maxims, and this suggested a certain gullibility on her part, of which the doctor had taken advantage. It suggested to her that even if her plans made no sense, she could continue as if they had. She could fool herself. She could make a fool of herself.

Still angry, still in her nightgown, Vera rose from the vanity and stepped out of the house.

❀   ❀   ❀

The moon rose above the fields, and in the weird time that lifted her up and carried her along, the moon sailed quickly across the sky. She walked toward the tree that her brother had planted until the moon, again, was stuck in its branches, looking like it wanted down. She continued walking, away from the farm and into the night. She wondered again about this J. E. Fuller, the author of her manual. She wondered about the kind of company he kept. Why did he lie to her? And who was this Zadoc Xenophone? A real person? And why could he not view "bright new moons"?

She stopped in her tracks. No. No, it was just nonsense. That's all it was, and so she walked again, but she could not seem to put the puzzle out of her mind.

Zadoc cannot view "bright new moons" because there is no such thing as that, because new moons are dark. Okay, she'd solved that part of the puzzle.

But then why did the doctor suggest that it might be possible for Vera Montague to see them? The doctor leaves the question open, unanswered. "Zadoc Xenophone cannot view bright new moons. Can Vera Montague?" It might be possible.

So maybe it's not nonsense, after all. Perhaps this is simply a way for the doctor to suggest that Vera is special. That she has rare powers. She can even view things that no one else can. For Vera Montague, anything is possible—or at least it isn't out of the question.

Okay. Vera was relieved. The phrase wasn't nonsense after all. It made an odd kind of sense, but it wasn't nonsense.

She stopped again, noticing that she was in an open field, the fresh plowed dirt feeling soft beneath her. She looked at her bare feet and laughed. It was a good thing Holly and Henry couldn't see her like this. They'd think she was crazy, but the fresh dirt felt so good against her feet.

Standing there, Vera admired the fullness of the moon, and she wondered at the fact that this was the same moon that everyone saw everywhere. Maybe Charlie was looking at it, even at this moment. Because it was the same moon, always circling, always changing, even if it never closed upon the center. Three-quarters, one-quarter, inching toward its absence like a nonsense phrase in the doctor's book.

For Charlie, this moon would come up maybe two hours later. Maybe more. Maybe, tonight, he was on a ship or standing at land's end. Maybe he could see this moon breaking apart upon the ocean waves.

"Maybe . . ."

Vera never thought of it before, but "maybe" was a strange word, a powerful word. She said it over and over until it seemed like a nonsense word.

"Nonsense . . ."

Suddenly Vera had a powerful feeling that there was no such thing as nonsense. She said the word over and over, until Nonsense was a dead god. Sense was all around her. There was nothing but sense, the cool night, the scattered stars, Charlie's tree stretching its limbs as if it were just waking up.

And what, now, was happening to the moon?

Clearly, it had been full until now, but now the moon was dark, like an eclipse, like an empty glass of milk. But, even so, she could see it plainly, a bright new moon. She closed her eyes and she could still see it. She could see the earth lining up between the sun and moon in space, as if she were watching this from a planet no one knew was there. She could see that the earth had a long dark shadow, a skirt that briefly caught the moon within its fold.

Even when she opened her eyes, she could see this moon, dark and withdrawn, solitary and complete. She could see this new moon as plainly as she could see the years ahead, a future that she could compose out of her book of spells, her numbers and letters, and her machine.

She could remember the future.

Tomorrow she would have a fight with Henry.

Well. No astounding display of intuition there! But she knew now how the fight would turn out, because there would be nothing Henry could do to stop her, save from kicking her out of the house, and that would not look good. So she would win. And in a week, the men at the office would be astounded as she typed for them a tap-dance sonata. She could even picture their blank, astonished faces. They looked like new moons.

And maybe for a year or so, she would do their books and double as a telephone operator. Young children would put their chairs up to the box on the wall and crank the phone, and she would be the ghostly angel who reassured them that nothing, nothing at all would ever hurt them. Each week she would put her money in the bank, where it would multiply, like mushrooms growing in the dark.

And if Henry ever tried to vex her will, say, to send the girls to high school or even to college, she would do whatever she wanted anyway, because her money would speak louder than the roar of, say, a preacher's voice. She knew that a preacher's voice still roared in Henry's head, and maybe it would do him some good to have something louder than that voice.

And if the girls brought children into the world, their lives would be different, because they would come from a powerful clan. They would learn spells from books, whatever those books might be. Mathematical spells. Alphabetical spells. With these spells, they would have the ability to transform the world. If the world around them did not suit them, they could create another—easily!

And these were only the ordinary things that would happen. There would be many more things, extraordinary things, things that she could not yet imagine. For instance, if ever Charlie's tree should be harvested, she would slice it up into a million pages. She would write a spell on each of those pages and send them circling around the world. And the first spell she would cast would be the one to bring her brother home, at least for a visit. As she walked back to the farm, she wrote her first letter to her brother in the dark new fragments that she juggled in her head.

It read, "Dear Charlie, I regret to inform you of the death of Nonsense."

And in immediate reply, Charlie's tree telegraphed the night wind through its branches, shivering in anticipation for whatever Vera would think of next.

She started another letter. "Dear Charlie," she wrote. "If our senses ever leave us, do not despair. Because from then on we will make sense."

This message swept away from her, shooting across the dark land. Soon, a large bird returned with an answer. She saw it swoop in from the night, quickly reading the message of her footprints in the blank plowed fields, and then the bird took off again, carrying the message: "Everything has changed!"

"But I am getting ahead of myself," she wrote. "It's so difficult to hold yourself back when the future rushes into your head. Let me start at the beginning. . . ." Later she would type the letter out, and it would assume the sharp authority of print.

"Dear Charlie . . ."

She breathed in. The soil pushed up between her toes.

Nonsense was dead. Her senses were alive.

She possessed a new machine, and it could cast spells.

"You would never guess what happened today. . . ."

The Gothenburg Marching Band

WE WERE THE LOUSIEST marching band in Nebraska, but the last person to figure that out was Mr. Jenke, our band director. He kept hauling us all over the place and begging people to let us march through their towns. We always figured he was too big to be a band director anyway, about six foot seven, and his arms hung down to his knees and flew all over the place, knocking over music stands, making the sheet music fly. Once he knocked a clarinet right out of a girl's mouth. He'd count out loud and spit, too, especially during crescendos, but we couldn't help but like him sometimes because we all felt kind of sorry for him.

The main trouble with Mr. Jenke was that he'd get these ideas at the last minute, just before he forced us to march out at half time or something. He'd say, Okay, trumpets, instead of turning right at measure 36, turn left for two measures and then turn right, and it'd end up looking like a pinball game. It was bad enough in concert band. Once, we did the "Warsaw Concerto," and he dragged out a P.A. system just before the concert without telling anyone and stuck the mike right inside the piano. He almost got sued over that one. But when it came to marching season, then he really got out of hand. He forced us to go to harvest festivals and county fairs, all that. He even forced us to go to the Frontier Days out in Cheyenne, Wyoming. We drove there all the way from Gothenburg just to make fools of ourselves.

You should have seen us. We kept bunching up and tripping over each other's heels because we had to march in place about forty-eight times. The float ahead of us kept stalling out, so we tried to march a little slower, but that's hard to do when you've been trained to take exactly eight steps every five yards. That's moving exactly twenty-two and a half inches per step, and the stupid drummers only knew one cadence. They were drummers only because they couldn't carry a tune, couldn't think of one if you asked them, and they didn't even care. If they weren't in band, they'd be in the reform school.

But then it was really weird. When we went past the judges' stand, we were all marching in perfect formation, toes pointed, everyone in step, ranks straight on the horizontal, vertical, and diagonal. A total fluke. Every single step was exactly, I mean exactly, twenty-two and a half inches. We'd never ever marched like that before in our lives. Of course, we weren't playing any music at the time. No way could we play music and march that well all at once. We just marched to the cadence and scooted past that judges' stand as fast as we could, and almost like that everyone started passing out, which is what comes of wearing wool dress uniforms when it's like a hundred degrees out and you're blowing "There Is No Place Like Nebraska" for about five miles. The first one to pass out was this anemic trombone player, but we all thought she was just showing off. But then it was like a chain reaction. A tuba went down, two French horns, a flute, another trombone. All the drummers stood around and smirked, but Mr. Jenke lost his head and screamed at all of us to do something.

As far as Mr. Jenke being there to help you in an emergency, just forget it. We had all these horn blowers down for the count, and the woodwinds falling over them, and the drummers standing there and just laughing about it, and Mr. Jenke turning every which way and just standing there. Thank God for the Fecht brothers. They started grabbing Coca-Colas out of the spectator's hands and dumping them on the casualties. Those Fechts probably saved our lives. But the thing of it is that as soon as we got to the rodeo, deciding to put this out of our minds, we heard the rodeo announcer say over the loudspeaker that we got third place, so we sneaked out of town that night before anyone figured it out. We sneaked out with a trophy. The only trouble was that Mr. Jenke didn't know it had been a big mistake. He started to think that we were state champion caliber. So then he signed us up for the Nebraska State Marching Band Competition, a big deal. Thousands and thousands of people showed up for it.

We tried to talk him out of it, but it didn't do any good. Pretty soon he started coming to school with charts and graphs and battle plans. They were all pretty amazing, X's and circles and figure eights all going into a tailspin. He was going to have us play "Aquarius," "with a Latin flavor," he said. He was going to have us start out with the theme music for *Two Thousand and One: A Space Odyssey*. And then we were going to end up with Elvis Presley's "Viva Las Vegas"—"for the kids in the audience," Mr. Jenke said. It looked pretty grim. All we could do at that point was try to convince everyone we knew to stay far, far away. At least then we'd only make fools of ourselves in front of strangers.

Every day, he had us kick-dancing and sidestepping and marching backward and doing three-quarter turns, and even hopping once in a while, and there were a lot of collisions and who knows how many near misses. One day he tried to make us march after an ice storm and people were slipping and slitting their lips on their mouthpieces, and a couple people almost knocked their front teeth out. But Mr. Jenke said he had everything planned, and nothing could go wrong. We figured that he'd even planned for how many casualties we could stand before we broke ranks and started to run. But, you know, it shouldn't be any surprise that we got better and better. We started believing we were a whole lot better than we were. That's the worst part. Of course, our folks didn't help things any, because they thought we were the best marching band in the world, and that's only part of the reason why you just can't trust anyone who loves you. We marched through leaves, we marched through snow, and we finally stopped complaining because we were numb. And then there came that one morning when we all got up about four o'clock and got ready for the long ride.

The drummers had spent the night with hypodermic needles, injecting oranges with vodka. The trumpet-and-trombone guys were all looking pretty beat up, because they'd played a football game the night before. When they were forty points behind, our boys begged the coach just to let them give up, but he wouldn't, no way. That coach was another story. Anyway, they all looked like they were hoping to die in their sleep. The clarinets arrived with this blue paint on their faces and curlers on, like they planned this ahead of time. And everyone was there except for Mr. Jenke, so we all stared at each other. We couldn't get over how nasty and ugly everyone looked at that time of the morning. It was like we hadn't ever seen each other before.

Finally, Mr. Jenke came squealing up in his Rambler with a huge banner sticking out the window and about three marching kettledrums in his trunk. The kettledrums were for our "Two Thousand and One" number, he said. He also picked up a few marching French horns, too. You know, the kind that stick out straight instead of curling around and back. We hadn't ever seen these things before, and we sure didn't know how to play them, but Mr. Jenke kept mumbling about how sharp we'd look. He said we could practice on the bus. We all thought he stole them from somewhere, because he wouldn't say where he got them.

On the way down to Lincoln, he had a tape recording of us playing. It was just a racket. Maybe it was only a bad recording, but we never figured we sounded that bad. And then he claimed that we didn't have time to get out and pee, so about the time we got to Kearney, we started to shout at him like we were dying, but he wouldn't listen. You'd be

surprised how fierce those girls were by the time we got to Grand
Island. A couple of them went up to the front of the bus and acted like
they were just going to force the driver over to the side of the road. All
the drummers were at the back of the bus, grinning at this whole thing,
grinning at everything. They'd been at those oranges and peeing into
Seven-Up bottles and trying to pass them off to a preacher's kid they
regularly picked on.

By the time we got to Aurora there was a mutiny. We started yelling,
"Let us out! Let us out!" and rocking the bus back and forth. Finally Mr.
Jenke told the bus driver to pull into a truck stop, and the girls stood in
line, and the guys just peed on the wheels. The drummers went inside
the gift shop and robbed the place blind. Each of them had these tiny
brown beer mugs, and they were drinking something out of them.
Maybe they just put pop in those mugs, but they pretended it was something else, and maybe it was, because back on the bus a half hour later,
one of the drummers was starting to throw up. The other drummers just
mocked him, imitating the sounds he was making. They didn't feel
sorry for him at all. We all threw open the windows and let the cold air
slide in, and Mr. Jenke didn't have a clue what was going on. Maybe he
was concentrating on our performance.

We got to Lincoln in about six hours. Mr. Jenke herded us down this
ramp into the huge basement where there were about three or four or
five dozen marching bands, maybe two or three or four thousand kids
all tuning up and practicing their music and getting dressed and marching in place. Mr. Jenke was scared. As soon as he saw all these bands, he
froze and started to shake and shout out, "Get those boys off the beach!
They're just piling up on the beach!" One of the Fecht boys grabbed
him and gave him a shake, but he was plain out of his head, a lot farther than we thought he could go. But, finally, at least he knew where
he was. He ordered us to get into our uniforms, and then he told us we
couldn't lie down or even sit down because we'd wrinkle them, and we
weren't due to go on for another four hours, so we tried to find the
same note to get ourselves in tune but we got no closer than this awful-
sounding chord. Mr. Jenke said, "That's close enough!" and then he
marched us in place and ran us through our routine about a dozen
times. He was slicing through the air with this new baton he'd just
bought, so we tried to stand back from him, but he kept moving in closer. He was swinging his arms and knocking people's hats off. One of the
drummers caught an elbow in the temple, and he went down, and that
anemic trombone player passed out, and the drum majorette started to
cry. We marched in place for almost the whole four hours. There were
seventy other school fight songs in that room, battling it out. Finally,

Mr. Jenke looked at his watch and screamed, "We're on! We're on!" He pushed us down this hallway that smelled like old towels, until we were in a dark and quiet place, and we knew we were next.

We could see the band that was ahead of us doing their routine. They were from Omaha, and they had two ranks filled with nothing but drums. They had four tom-toms and five kettledrums, and they twirled their sticks. We all glared at our drummers, because they were going to be the death of us, but those drummers didn't even look like they knew where we were. They were all leaning against each other, trying to get some rest. Meanwhile, the Omaha band started high-stepping and leaning clear back. Mr. Jenke was watching them, too, and thinking about something, which is always dangerous, and then he gathered us around him for our pep talk.

"Okay," he said. "We are going to do things a little differently." We all moaned. "Shut up!" he said. "It's just gonna be a small change. Instead of marching out like usual, we're going to play 'Ach, du lieber Augustin' and goose-step out, okay? It'll be cute. And then we'll play 'Two Thousand and One.' And then when we get to 'Viva Las Vegas,' we'll high-step, just like those guys out there, okay? Just lean back and pump those legs high!"

"No, no, no!" we said.

"Shut up!" Mr. Jenke said. "It's gonna look sharp!"

We tried to talk him out of it, but it was too late. The Omaha band was already marching off, and the lights were going down to get ready for our performance.

Now the only people who knew how to play "Ach, du lieber Augustin" were the trumpets and tubas, just because they like to cornball around in the band room. They'd worked out harmonies and everything, but they'd never played that song in public. But what stunk was our goose-stepping. By the time we'd finished, no one was in the right place for "Two Thousand and One," so we all had to shuffle around a bit. The lights flashed on bright just as we started blasting out "Two Thousand and One," and for the first time we saw how big that auditorium was and how many people were there, just like dots in a newspaper photograph. And the trumpets went Blaaaaa! Blaaaaa! Blaaaaaa! . . . Bla-BLAAAAAAAAAA! And the drummers went nuts on the kettledrums. BOOM-boom! BOOM-boom! BOOM-boom! BOOM-boom! BOOM-boom! BOOM-boom! And then the tubas went BOOOOOOOOOOO! But we just sounded like a little dog, barking in a big empty corn bin.

That's exactly how we sounded, and if a band can't make "Two Thousand and One" sound big, it can't do anything. And then so many things went wrong after that, nobody even wanted to think about it afterward. There were so many echoes in that big auditorium that nobody knew who was playing what or when, and we got off tempo, and when one of the majorettes stuck our her arms, her zipper came zipping down her back, because her outfit was too tight, and she ran off the floor, and then the drummers—damn those drummers, anyway! The drummers got turned around so they were always marching just the opposite way from what they should have been marching, and we were dodging each other, and then we were finished, and there was hardly any applause, and we couldn't even figure out how to get off the floor. We just stood there in the silence and stared at each other until Mr. Jenke grabbed one of the drummers by the scruff of the neck, and he hauled that drummer off the floor with his feet kicking, and we all just followed.

To make matters worse, the next band came out and did one of those kaleidoscope routines that you see the June Taylor Dancers do on Jackie Gleason. We crawled up into the high bleachers where no one could see us. We watched them from up there, and Mr. Jenke thought they were so good that he practically bawled. During supper, we all tried to talk Mr. Jenke into taking us home, but he said he was going to make us stay around for the awards ceremony like it was some kind of punishment. So we had to sit around and watch all these bands get "superiors" and "excellents," and listen to all those kids stand up and scream like they'd just won a million dollars, and then it came around to us and we got a "good," and the dim-witted clarinets stood up and screamed, and Mr. Jenke told them to shut up and sit down and not call attention to us, because the awards didn't go any lower than "good."

After that, we just wanted the marching band season to be over. The only trouble was that we had one more engagement. We were supposed to march in Brady, Nebraska, for the Brady Days. It was stupid. Brady has only about two hundred people, hardly enough to line the parade route for a city block. But they didn't want to admit that, so the parade route stretched out, winding back and forth through town, probably so nobody in Brady would have to step off their porch.

So we drove down to Brady and formed our ranks and marched along, with no one even around to watch us, drumsticks clicking on the rims, trombones and trumpets and clarinets silent. Mr. Jenke marched along beside us in his special director's uniform, but his legs were so long that he kept scooting ahead of us and then he'd turn around and scowl like he expected us to catch up. We waited for the drums to get around to playing the roll-off, but there was no one to even play to. We made a wagon-wheel corner onto a side street. We didn't even have a trail of fresh horse manure to follow.

Finally we saw someone, some man with his head under a car hood. He looked up at us, his face smudged with grease, so we got the roll-off and played him "On Wisconsin!" He grinned and wiped his hands on an oil rag, so he'd have clean hands to applaud us with. We made another wagon-wheel corner just in time to see the horse-and-banner team a block ahead of us before they turned on to another street. A bunch of old folks had dragged their rockers out on the front lawn, and they started to applaud just as soon as they saw us, even before we started to play. So we played the "Notre Dame Fight Song" and did our about-face-and-cut-back-through-the-ranks routine. God, you should have seen those old folks. They were amazed. Of course, we had to do it again to get going back the way we were originally, and they just about went nuts. They didn't stop applauding for a second.

At the next corner, there was no one except this kid who stood up and said, "They went that way!" In appreciation, we stood there and marched in place while we played that soul song "The Horse." The trumpets and trombones just loved that song. They yapped right through it, trying to play it faster than the rest of the band, just showing off. Then we got to the next corner and did a spinning three-quarter left turn and went marching to the south. A dog was standing there, panting a bit and looking like he was trying to think up something nasty to do. Then we marched on a bit more and noticed that the pavement had turned to gravel. We marched some more and noticed that we'd left the city limits and were marching down a country road with no houses, no trees, just a barbed-wire fence with these three bay horses standing there watching us. The clarinets and flutes almost fell out of rank to go over and pet them. But they didn't. You could tell they wanted to, though.

So we marched on about a mile or so and came up to another corner and marched in place for a while as Mr. Jenke tried to figure out whether to turn left or right or just turn around and go back or what. The most sensible thing would be to turn around, but all of a sudden Mr. Jenke got stubborn, I suppose because he didn't want us to know how lost he really was. So we took a left and marched on about another mile into the country. If you cranked your head around you could see the town of Brady getting farther and farther away. Some of the kids started moaning, but Mr. Jenke wouldn't listen.

We all figured there was something going on in his life to make him do this to us. Whatever it was we never heard about it. He just made us march. A hawk sat on an old telephone pole that was leaning out of a ditch and glared at us like we were intruders. The gravel road got bumpier. There was grass growing in the middle, and then there were just a couple wheel ruts, and then even those wheel ruts vanished, and we were marching through somebody's pasture.

All of a sudden, Mr. Jenke whipped around. He was marching backward, his cap low over his eyes. He looked real serious, and he blew one long whistle and three short ones, and we started playing "Viva Las Vegas" and high-stepping, which made a lot of sense right then, because the grass was getting really long. We played about as good as we ever did. We all wished that there'd been someone there to watch us, aside from those cows. They just stood and stared at us like they figured this was supposed to mean something, but they couldn't figure out what. We marched over a hill and across another pasture. Mr. Jenke didn't act like he was proud of us at all, but he must have been, because we kept in formation and didn't break ranks, not even when a bunch of quail bolted out of the brush, their wing tips clapping just like mad.

The Dirty Shame Hotel

DR. ORRIN SHUFFLED in and took his spot in the hideous green chair in the lobby, where the setting sun made his face look more jaundiced than it already was. He coughed into his handkerchief, soiled from days of use, and took out his pipe and his journal. Humming and puffing, he contemplated the new tenant, a skinny boy in baggy shorts. Evidently, everything the boy owned was in his duffel bag, which he clutched to his chest.

"Ten a night," repeated the concierge. The boy took off his shoe and picked a five and five ones out of the toe. The concierge counted the bills twice before he said, "You'll be in 104."

"Ah, the suicide suite," said Dr. Orrin. "Last abode of the poet Polanski. You poor boy."

The boy made his way toward the staircase.

"Fevers and chills, that's what that room holds! Sweaty sheets!"

The boy ignored him, and in this way discovered at least one of the house rules right off the bat.

"That Polanski, a witty devil he was. Didn't want to give him any sass, no sir! Why, he'd whip around and give you a piece of his mind in iambic pentameter! He was no one to mess with, no sir! I remember when he came over to my flat, saying that he needed an eraser. First time. He never needed an eraser before, because he mainly worked in the oral tradition and usually forgetfulness was enough—"

But the boy was already gone. Dr. Orrin waited in silence for his next victim, not bothering with the concierge, who feigned deafness the way Dr. Orrin's estranged wife had feigned sleep. The next tenant darted in, out of breath and looking over his shoulder. He held a bulging sack in his fist and produced the two hundred dollars for a month's rent much too quickly. That immediately drew out Dr. Orrin's suspicions. The concierge handed over a key.

"Ah! Room 105, a good choice! The room of the famous Matthew La Boe, student of human nature, actor extraordinaire, and criminal by circumstance. I remember the night La Boe came to me, saying, 'Doc? Ya gotta help me.' You see, La Boe's great talent as an actor led him to—"

The man whipped around and said a guttural, foreign-sounding word. Only after the man went up the stairs did Dr. Orrin speak again. "I'd watch that one, I would." The concierge said nothing. "I *said*, I'd be *vigilant* about the client in 105!" As usual, the concierge did not reply, so Dr. Orrin turned back to his daily journal, which was always patient, always interested in what he had to say.

Slowly the sounds of the street sneaked into the Dirty Shame Hotel like a penniless vagabond that, seeing the establishment didn't notice its presence, invited in its rude friends: the sounds of traffic, the voices of pedestrians, a baby crying, a faraway sound of a bar band playing a crude and repetitious song. Then, sensing no resistance, a mob of noises burst in: a vomiting commuter jet, the clacking and hissing of the radiators, a full-throated motorcycle, and finally—right above the lobby—the sudden racket of a room full of jumping chairs. . . .

"Rachel and Sam, going at it again," Dr. Orrin said out loud. "A marriage made in Valhalla. I remember when Sam came to me begging for advice. Rachel was abusing him, although not so as to leave any marks, but he did not know how to defend himself and—"

The concierge left the room abruptly, but that didn't stop Dr. Orrin. After relighting his pipe, he finished the story by writing it down in front of his own audience, disappointed not to have another interruption.

❊   ❊   ❊

At the Dirty Shame Hotel, night descended like a kind of dread. Even though the crickets in the walls gave the place the feel of a country inn, the hotel stood in a dangerous neighborhood, the windows draped in chain mail, the streets patrolled by blowing trash. After 1 A.M., the doors were locked to all except those most ancient and familiar hookers who had lost the copyright to their sex, having let it pass into the public domain. Night was less a time of the day than a kind of depression, a sinking feeling that contained those twenty roomers like a dream that something terrible was bound to happen. They could die in their sleep. They could wake up and wonder where they were. They could walk out, one by one, to the edge of a personal abyss and—really only intending to take a look down—could slip.

"You disgust me," Rachel Bullock said, in a low and threatening voice. "I cannot tell you how sick I feel to have your tongue slithering in my mouth." Sam was a small but muscular man, huddled silently in a great, soft chair that made him look even smaller. "You smell bad. You don't keep yourself clean. And you fart under the sheets," said Rachel. Sam could not disagree. He was chronically flatulent, even more so when he ate cabbage, which he loved to eat. "The idea of having sex with you makes me want to vomit," said Rachel.

Disagreeing with her only extended these moments of siege, so Sam usually kept silent, waiting for her finally to grow tired. But tonight Sam's plan wasn't going to work. Sam could see the blood vessels bulging at Rachel's temples when she said, "Speak up, coward! We're gonna have it out once and for all!" She faked a punch at his face, and he flinched. She faked another and suckered him again, which she found comical. All through the hotel, the pathetic clientele could hear her throaty smoker's laugh.

Among those who listened was the boy in the baggy shorts, whose name was Jerry Hauser. His room was right below the Bullocks, and Rachel's voice boomed through the heating ducts. But the odd thing was that he was strangely comforted by this argument, which among the strange sounds of the city—the faraway sirens, the indiscreet gurgle of someone else's toilet, the phlegmatic sleep of Dr. Orrin—among all these sounds, this sound was familiar. It reminded him of home. And although he was, in part, a roomer in this hotel to get away from home, he needed the familiar sound of a familial argument to lull him to sleep.

Lawrence Rafi, who sometimes went by the name of Lorenzo Raphael, lay on his back with a stranger beside him, smiling to himself. He was blowing smoke rings into the air, enjoying the sound of his sometime lover Rachel abusing her husband. Part Pakistani, he often passed himself off as Italian or occasionally as a Gypsy. He was the solitary hunter of last calls in bars, able to spot the one woman in the crowd who was ill at ease with her escort, or who wanted vengeance, or who enjoyed participating in displays of cruel indifference. From the mustache and the butter-slick hair he so carefully combed, one might think that he was in love with himself, but he was not. In fact, he hated himself with an absolute gravity that would make most men buckle. When he said to his many lovers, "We deserve each other," they always took it as a compliment. But he only meant that his lovers were the baleful image of himself. And yet he felt happy as only the undivided truly are. Knowing himself had become his final excuse, and he knew himself without apology. Snubbing out the cigarette, he picked up his bedside reading matter, a book entitled *Sexual Addiction*. He chuckled softly as he read, like a man who was reading a flattering feature story about himself in the Sunday paper.

Franz Meekham, Bachelor of Divinity, Master of Theology, circuit minister in the Bolgia of Incontinence, spent a good deal of that night, as every night, attempting to teach his bulldog how to kneel. This was difficult, because of the shortness of the bulldog's legs and also because of the dog's disposition. A stalwart animal, as bulldogs are in most things, the dog was lax when it came to religion. Perhaps this had to do with the dog's anatomy. Meekham had personally witnessed cattle kneeling and horses kneeling—and he knew from his religious study that camels could kneel. But dogs? Never. So often—Meekham thought—so very often it is that those who are faithful in the world of men are faithless when it comes to God. "Kneel, Theo! Kneel!" the Reverend Meekham said, pulling the dog's legs from behind. The dog stretched out and rolled to her back, panting and exposing her belly in canine wantonness and submission, seeming to invite the reverend to make love to her. Scandalized, Reverend Meekham slapped the animal and went about his prayers without her.

After all movement in the halls ceased, the criminal in 105 peered into his sinister sack, laughing softly, counting. From the sack there issued a clicking sound, a mechanical relative of the crickets in the wall. He spread his loot out on the balding carpet: a hundred watches, all of them filched from the bodies of the dead. This was the criminal's calling—to attend funerals, to mix in with the crowd of mourners, to assume with great finesse the traditional postures of grief, to stand at the open caskets as if contemplating this unbearable breech, and then—with quick fingers—to unburden the corpse of these useless measurements of time and decay. It amazed the crook how many stiffs were buried with their watches. A watch more often than a cross went into the earth to accompany the corpse on its dread journey. How useless. How insane. Although he sold these watches to the living when he could, the crook never thought that he was a crook. Sometimes, he thought he stole watches on instinct. Often he stole them with the best of intentions. But, finally, he didn't really know why he stole them. The reasons for his compulsion escaped him, tormented him.

Usually, no one noticed the missing watches, not even members of the family. But today, no sooner had the criminal liberated the dead man from his timepiece than the next mourner cried out in outrage, accusing the bewildered funeral director, "What did you do with his watch, Ghoul?" The funeral director, so contaminated by his years of faked sympathy, blustered out his innocence but lacked all credibility. Meanwhile, the panicked criminal slipped out, the watch beating so loudly in his pocket as he ran down the street that, after fetching his collection from a locker in the bus station, he sought refuge in the Dirty Shame Hotel.

Of course, this was not the hotel's real name. This was the name given to the place by the dead poet Polanski. In fact, the only person who referred to the hotel by this name, and at that never aloud, was the good doctor Charles Orrin, who after a brief sleep was passing another wakeful night. He was composing his memoirs. He had already written about his prodigious youth, the confluence of his many ideas, the witless academies that fearfully rejected his conceptual revolution. He had already described the explosion of his grand theory upon the public domain, and how the public turned against him. After wandering for many years and many chapters, he finally arrived at the Dirty Shame Hotel, and that's where he was tonight:

"The very night of my arrival, the heavens opened up to show their pleased satisfaction in a brilliant display of northern lights. Shimmering snakes of light, glowing condors stretched out their wings, and I knew then that this place, this hotel so badly regarded in the community, was my seat of power. Here I could continue my work, bringing my disparate musings into a unified vision—and finally my theory, which seemed so threatening when it was nakedly presented to the public, would find the rich clothing it needed so that the public could look at it without searing their eyes."

At that moment, a sharp pain stabbed through the doctor's side, moving up to his armpit, around his back, and up into his head. He chomped so tightly on his pipe that he could almost hear the crunching of the stem. With difficulty, he stood up from his writing desk and stumbled over to his Murphy bed, placing his pipe in its perch on the bed stand before he succumbed to the unblinking honesty that only pain can unleash. Every word that came to him was like a black drop slowly dripping into a black, black pool that reflected everything the way it was.

In the morning, feeling better, glad to have survived another night, Dr. Orrin wandered into the distressing café that filled up the street side of the Dirty Shame Hotel. Immediately he saw the boy, Jerry Hauser, sitting on a stool at the freckled counter. He took a seat next to him.

"Permit me to introduce myself. I am Dr. Charles W. Orrin. Perhaps you've heard of me? The Orrin Effect?" Jerry really didn't say no or yes, but he made the mistake of looking the doctor in the eye. "You're surprised? Yes, many are. Not many are able to become so famous while they still move and breathe. Yes, I am still alive. Although I had a difficult bowel movement this morning." The boy rotated on the stool, imagining for a moment that he was a camera panning the room. "Oh, yes. I have suffered in the name of science. My wife thought I was sick to dwell on such sad things. After divorcing me, she fought savagely to keep our children from seeing me. I don't blame her. The children experienced frightful torments at school. Cruel teasing. Most everyone felt I was trying to project my own deviance on the until-then-happy world, and thereby to obscure my own abnormality. Such are the sacrifices. Such is the bitter fate of the teller-of-truth. Even the cold cynics of the human condition thought I was being cruel for the sake of cruelty." Dr. Orrin sighed. "I was young and idealistic. I thought that I could save the world if they but knew the demon's name, if they would only understand the vectors of the massive infection that had rooted in their veins. I had no mission other than relief of the rash that no one failed to scratch and spread, not knowing it was there. I thought that they would appreciate my discovery. How foolish of me."

The boy looked at him. "What did you discover?" Since he was trapped, he might as well play along.

"Why, the Orrin Effect," the doctor said. "I didn't name the thing myself. No, the horrible thing in the scientific world is that when you discover something awful—" Dr. Orrin paused and lowered his voice. "Well, then, they name it after you. . . ."

"But what is it?"

"Don't they teach you anything at school?" The doctor sighed again and brought out his pipe. "Perhaps you are too young to know." He tapped out the pipe on his heel. "Perhaps the world wasn't ready to know—but truth waits for no one, boy. Although sometimes I wish the truth were not so painfully clear to me. It goes off like a bullet in my head."

Dr. Orrin stared contemplatively at the blackboard showing the day's special, as a slouching, sickly-looking man with a healthy, mean-looking bulldog walked in. The doctor studied the man. "Have you had the opportunity and good fortune to meet the Reverend Meekham?" The boy shrugged. "Reverend!" Dr. Orrin boomed out. "Come over and meet my young friend—?"

The doctor looked at Jerry, expecting him to fill in his name.

"Bob," Jerry said.

"My young friend Bob. Come here and give us a show. What's the word for this morning, Reverend?"

"Sin," the reverend said, without hesitation.

"And?"

"And wages."

"Good, very good!" the doctor said, with enthusiasm.

"The sin of . . . wages!" the reverend said.

"Very good!"

"The sin of wages is . . . *death!*" the reverend proclaimed.

"I see it clearly now. You've thrown a spotlight on the part of the stage where there was nothing before but darkness! It makes me wonder how I hadn't seen it before." The reverend made his way out into the gray city light, with the bowlegged bulldog trotting behind. "Interesting man," Dr. Orrin said. "A missionary for years, subject to all kinds of torture. Probably saved by his own stupidity. He was in Borneo, I believe, where the local witch doctor thrust a totem of fertility in the reverend's face. Offended, the reverend struck the idol out of the witch doctor's hands, and by this the tribesmen immediately recognized the reverend's holiness, abusing the gods to honor the abuses men have suffered. If he'd respected the idol, as many liberal ministers might have, he would have been quickly put to death. Such is the luck of the true imbecile. And a true example of the Orrin Effect."

Dr. Orrin stared sadly at the blackboard, probably contemplating the lucklessness of his own genius. "I say to you," said the doctor. "The Meekhams of the world shall inherit the earth! So Bob. Do you have enough money for your breakfast?" Jerry Hauser hesitated to answer, not knowing what the doctor's generosity would oblige him to. "Oh, I see that you are a proud young man. Good for you! But you must put your pride behind you and allow me to buy you your first meal of the day. Then we might have strength to resume this conversation."

And that was the devil's bargain that the boy, by his silence, accepted.

❈　　❈　　❈

To say that everyone in the hotel ate at this dangerous little café, with its fly-flecked windows, its coffee like a South American coup, its deep-fat fryers full of the memory of tastes as long-lasting as the most bitter of grudges, would be an exaggeration. However, it was against the house rules to cook in the rooms, so many inhabitants found themselves forced to eat there, and many more passed through the restaurant on their way to the street. One of these drifters was the criminal in 105, who stopped to sniff the air like a cornered animal.

"Excuse me," Dr. Orrin said to him. "Do you happen to have the time?"

The criminal glared at the doctor—how much did he know? "I don't carry a watch," the criminal said. This was the truth. The criminal always went out to hunt bare-wristed.

"I don't blame you," Dr. Orrin said. "The burden of time always slows one down. Time itself is dangerous. It is no wonder that the Chronos of mythology devours his children. Indeed, how we regard time often verges on the ridiculous!"

Almost against his will, the criminal found himself interested by this point of view, which seemed sympathetic to the vague urges of his own.

"Allow me to give you a brief disquisition. First off, why do we count the new day as beginning at midnight, when the numbers are continuous for another fifty-nine minutes? By all rights, the new day should begin at one. Or, if we are somehow accustomed to the hour, either by habit or superstition, then by all rights the new day, midnight, should be recorded as zero. And yet, this is merely one example of our senseless attitudes about time."

Agitated by the truth of the old man's words, the criminal forced himself to walk away. To hear these words was like putting a finger right on his sore. It was too painful, too real.

"A rude man, and a sneak," Dr. Orrin said. Once again he brooded upon the ingratitude of people who would not accept his wisdom, but as if the world were attempting to confuse this issue, a woman appeared and issued a clarion call of feigned affection.

"Dr. Orrin!" the woman cried. "Good morning!"

The boy was startled to hear that the same harsh voice he'd heard last night, which was so much like his mother's voice, was this morning clothed in the sweetest of flesh. He felt an erection stirring and crossed his legs.

"How are you?" Rachel asked Dr. Orrin. "Are you feeling well? Are you writing?"

"Writing? Yes. Feeling well? Passably. Sometimes when I am about to go to sleep I have the strong impression of falling. A most unpleasant sensation, called by some a myoclonic jerk. It makes my rest fitful."

"And who is the handsome young man with you?"

"This is . . . Bob," the doctor said as Jerry blushed, the pressure building.

"Such a bright and shiny young man," Rachel said. "You'll have to watch him, doctor, or the weasels might come and steal him away."

Jerry didn't understand this, but he regarded the comment as a kind of threat. The pressure dropped.

"And how is your husband?" Dr. Orrin asked.

Rachel looked sad. "Such a burden," she said, "to be the strong one. Every day he comes home from work, defeated, and if I don't build him back up I'm afraid he won't be able to face another day."

"You're a marvel," said the doctor. "You're the only one in this hotel who will stop and give comfort to an old man. So many will judge one on exteriors, trapped as one is inside this uncompromising husk."

"Oh, doctor, I might have to visit you some night and teach you that you are not as old as you think." She hugged him, and then she violated the boy's boundaries by giving a pinch to his cheek, which stung. The boy wore that sting long after she'd left.

"One thing I will never understand, my boy," Dr. Orrin said. "And that is why God—if there is a God, and generally I believe that there is not, but if there is—why did God make young people so beautiful and old people so ugly? I will have to ask Reverend Meekham about that. But perhaps that's just another example of the Orrin Effect."

The boy felt a brief urge to ask the doctor to explain, but he suppressed it, wanting to get out and move around the city. He had to make another five dollars, at least, before nightfall.

"I have to leave now," the boy said.

"Yes, yes, of course," the doctor said, obviously disappointed. "You're young. You have a world to conquer. Well, then. Go at it, my young friend. Good luck!"

Slowly the doctor was enveloped by his own immutable aura, sad to be alone and old and so irrevocably ugly.

❀   ❀   ❀

Samuel Bullock was lucky enough to work the day shift at a bread factory. About his daily defeats, Rachel was wrong. As the chemically sweetened odor of dough drifted over the city, he felt he was giving everyone a universal blessing. He had prestige. He could diagnose the ills of the ancient machines by the rhythms of the sounds they made. He felt that as soon as he stepped into the building that housed the massive kneading machines and the ovens, his heart and his breathing aligned themselves to this rhythm. Making bread was his religion.

So it hurt him daily to come home to the woman he loved and to hear how much he had disappointed her. More than hurt him, it bewildered him. His purity and innocence was, to her, an emblem of his weakness—as was his patient silence. To her, his constancy was a signature of his indecision. His religious devotion to making bread was a sign of his shortsightedness, and he thought that she knew him better than he did.

Lorenzo Rafi waited in his bed for Rachel to come to him, which she did, with regularity, Mondays, Wednesdays, and Fridays at noon. She came to him by a circuitous route, meant to deceive not only Samuel but also the eyes of the hotel, the old man Orrin. Knowing that Orrin would be taking his breakfast in the hotel café, she always made an appearance there first, about ten o'clock. After greeting him and fawning over him, she would go out the street side. For two hours she conducted her errands and generally wasted time, and then as noon approached she scaled the outside fire escape to Lorenzo's room, where she appeared outside his window as an angel of light, surrounded by the nimbus of greasy glass. Rising from the bed, naked, Lorenzo opened the window and, holding her waist with both hands, lowered her into the room, slowly, against his body.

"Larry," she murmured, in a voice that came from deep inside her.

As they made love, she spoke to him in an ordinary voice, sometimes reviewing lists of things she needed to get done, sometimes talking about the small, irritating things that had happened to her since they'd last made love. Sometimes she complained about her husband. Lorenzo didn't mind, since he made love to her from the depths of his own sexual solitude. And her distraction didn't seem to keep her from the racking orgasms that would start to come in a mounting chain reaction. Sometimes she counted them off. "That's three for me." She thought that he would want to know. But the truth is that he never listened to a word she said.

Dr. Orrin sat in the lobby, as a Vietnamese couple came in, seeming to argue. He couldn't tell. Their clipped voices sounded to him like the reports of small automatic weapons on a firing range. He was reading, that afternoon, the *International Journal of Lawsonomy*, to which he was a sometime contributor. But he set down the volume to listen to the Vietnamese, who seemed to be talking about duck tails, bad luck, clocks, mukluks, and the dying language, langue d'oc, seeming to interrupt each other's interruptions.

Dr. Orrin stood up, casually, and walked over to the front desk. The concierge stood there, in a world of his own. "Did I ever tell you about the time a delegation of Tibetan priests came to me, wanting my opinion on—"

The concierge immediately left, a reaction that the doctor had intended to provoke. He then took the opportunity to examine the guest register, seeing the boy listed there as Bob Jones. The doctor smiled. A solid name, it pleased him. He saw that the Vietnamese couple was registered under a name he did not dare to pronounce. But his real reason for checking the guest list was to see the name of the suspicious resident of room 105, the criminal. And there he saw the name "Matthew La Boe."

The name—which was in fact the name of the last crook to live there—pleased the doctor, providing additional evidence of the power of suggestion over the criminal mind. Now all he would have to do is observe the man, factor out his schedule, and find a safe time to investigate the room. He might have felt that this was a great feat, but as he walked back to his chair, a sudden insight depressed him. He recorded it in his journal:

"One would think that people who were blessed with good intuition would also be blessed by good luck, that they were in tune with secrets and hidden rhythms. But, alas, this was not so. Good intuition provoked the gods, if gods there be and generally I think there are not, to anger and jealousy. To be in tune with the universe was to invoke competition with the masters of destiny, who were bound to get even. Another example of the Orrin Effect."

After using Lorenzo's shower to take her second of the day, this one to remove the mad reek of her passion, Rachel left by way of the fire escape. Outside, she walked the street until her hair was dry and then she went back to the hotel, where once again she would flirt with Dr. Orrin in the lobby. To assist her in this pattern of deceit, Lorenzo might wander into the lobby himself, descending the stairs like a gentleman of great leisure, and inquire of the front desk if there was a message for him. She would ignore him, and he would ignore everyone, enveloping himself in a traveling circle of self-importance and indifference.

Often she was there to greet, or snub, her husband as he came in from work, his pale skin covered by a white dusting of flour. Because she worried about her general reputation, it was more important to her to deceive Dr. Orrin than to deceive her husband. Indeed, there were times when she delivered cruel hints to her husband, since she considered him too dumb to pick up on her infidelity otherwise. But for the doctor's sake, she often made a public show of affection, hugging her husband and smoothing his doughy hair. Perhaps the doctor was taken in. Often one does not question the deceitful aspects of those who make one feel good about oneself. And perhaps her husband knew the truth. Often the victims of deceit bind themselves in a contract with the liar, agreeing to play the part of the one who is being lied to. Samuel was grateful for any bit of affection he got. He knew that everyone in the hotel could hear them fight. So he wanted them to believe that they loved as fiercely.

Today, as Sam walked in, Rachel threw her arms around him, gushing, "Are you okay?" but seeming to suggest by her question that she doubted his potential to reach that very possibility. Okayness was beyond him.

"I feel great," he said. "I had a great day."

"Really?" Rachel gave the doctor a worried look and said to Sam, "Well, we can talk about it later."

"There's nothing to talk about. My day went fine."

"Poor dear," she said, glancing over at Lorenzo who was standing at the front desk. She thought he was listening in on what they said. He was, in fact, absorbed in reading a piece of mail. It was addressed to "Occupant."

❀   ❀   ❀

Jerry wandered down the street, past panhandlers, pawnshops, and street vendors, but none of these possible solutions were for him. He saw an old man, overdressed for the warm weather in a stocking cap and an army coat, pulling a shopping cart full of pop cans that were swarming with bees. Jerry thought about stopping the man and asking him where he traded in his cans, but he didn't have the courage. So for several hours he daydreamed about home, the memory of his mother stuffing up his head like a bad cold. At home, both anxiety and lodging were assured every night. He walked past a street musician, a man with a banjo, his case full of coins. Jerry listened to him play for several minutes, then tossed a quarter into his case. That left five quarters, two dimes, and a penny in his pocket and four dollar bills in the toe of his tennis shoe. He found another quarter in the street, so, feeling lucky, feeling any money spent would at least be replaced, he went into an air-conditioned café, intending to buy a soda, cool down, and think. As he stood at the cashier's counter, not able to see a place to sit down, the cashier asked him, "Are you the replacement?"

"Yes," Jerry said.

"Thank God," she said, and she led him back into the kitchen where plates and coffee cups were stacking up. She showed him how to run the dish machine, and Jerry washed dishes like a demon for three hours, after which the cashier came back, gave him a ten, and fired him.

On his way back to the hotel, Jerry found himself—without really being conscious of it—standing in front of a pawnshop, staring at an acoustic guitar. He had never played a guitar before, although when he listened to the radio, his fingers often ran over imaginary frets. Frequently he imagined himself playing to groups of good friends, their faces always darkened since he didn't have real friends.

When he got back to the hotel, Dr. Orrin was seated in the lobby, seeming to be waiting for him. "Ah, my good friend Bob. Did you have an eventful day?"

"Yes," Jerry said. "I'm okay now."

"A lucky day?"

"Yes," Jerry said.

"Oho, out to disprove my pessimistic philosophy?"

Jerry didn't know what to say. He shrugged.

"Well," Dr. Orrin said, "shouldn't you know what it is first, before you attempt to disprove it?" Jerry sat down, having nothing better to do. "First off," Dr. Orrin said, "you have to understand the physical science behind my theory. Could you, say, understand the Fall of the Roman Empire unless you understood gravity first? Not at all. And neither can you understand the Orrin Effect until you first understand the science of Lawsonomy."

"Lawsonomy," Jerry said.

"Yes, the universal countertheory of forces. Now, traditional science has never been able to link the forces governing the electromagnetic spectrum, that is light, with the laws covering the motion of planetary bodies, that is gravity, correct? So, therefore, how can they link these twin forces with the forces governing human nature? It's impossible. So without the primary link, a unified law governing both gravity and light, traditional science is stuck. It cannot, therefore, go on to the more ambitious task of discovering the physics of human desire. Lawsonomy does not have this problem, since it understands that both light and gravity work on the principle of suction."

"Suction," Jerry said.

"And desire does, too. Everything does."

"Okay."

"Now the Orrin Effect takes this idea and explores some of the contradictions it imposes on the human dilemma. Earlier today, I mentioned one of these contradictions. That is the idea that old people are ugly and young people are beautiful. Why should this be? It's an utter contradiction, according to Lawsonomy. Old age is obviously a sucker. The young are obviously sucked in to old age, correct? But beauty—the most splendid possession of the young—is also a sucker, and the beholder, longing for beauty, is sucked toward it. So how can the young be both the suckers and sucked? The answer to this seeming contradiction is the Orrin Effect. Do you follow so far?"

Jerry was thinking about playing guitar, but he caught the rising tone of the question and nodded his head.

"Brilliant boy! But perhaps I am going too fast. Verbal definitions are always complex, so allow me to define by example. Say you fall in love with someone because they are quiet. Soon this quiescence will set you to rage. The Orrin Effect! Fall in love with someone because they pay attention to you, and soon you will hate them for how they are smothering you. Love the young because they are beautiful? And soon your very love will turn them old and ugly. It's love itself that causes people to age. These are the very contradictions that the great Lawson overlooked,[1] because he assumed, wrongly, his cosmology to be in a constant state. And that is where the Orrin Effect steps in. The Orrin Effect states the contradictions of life that make it not worth living. It diagrams the dangerous ricochet of human desire. It explains the poetic injustice of rejection and utter

1. Alfred William Lawson, 1869-1955(?): physicist, economist, and pioneer professional baseball pitcher; inventor of the term "aircraft" as well as the first passenger plane; founder of the Direct Credits Society; Supreme Head and First Knowledgian of the Des Moines University of Lawsonomy. —The editor.

repulsion in a universe where the unifying principle is suction. I might add here that, according to the Orrin Effect, the very act of defining something alters it into its opposite, and thus we have—"

"I think I have to rest," Jerry said.

"Yes, of course," the doctor said.

"I have to rest," Jerry repeated, and after paying his ten dollars at the desk, he went upstairs to his room. Once again, night descended on the Dirty Shame Hotel. Or to use the terminology of Dr. Orrin and his great progenitor Lawson, the Dirty Shame Hotel sucked the night down, just as it sucked in the old and new customers. As the doctor would have noted, the Orrin Effect explained the natural evolution of a hotel from a clean, new, comfortable establishment that could not attract any customers into a run-down, shabby den of iniquities whose rooms were full almost every night.

Rachel Bullock understood the Lawsonian principles of suction better than most. She also understood the Orrin Effect, although she did not have the patience to hear this theory put into words. That night she released a volley of foul words at the vacuum where her husband reclined, sucking them in, quivering under the sheets. She scolded him until fatigue overcame her and she crawled into bed, where, hardly minutes later, she was irresistibly drawn to suck on his ear. She kissed his neck. Her face moved down his body to where his friendly little organ was waiting for her, begging. She had no desire for him, and so was obsessively drawn to quench his desire. The Orrin Effect.

At the Lizard's Lounge, a bar just down the street, the Lothario Lorenzo turned the deep wells of his vampire's eyes to the room, where the woman who detested him the most, who had noticed him out of all the other sad hunters in the crowd because her revulsion for him was utter and complete, was immediately sucked in. By loving him she could prove how completely she hated herself. The Orrin Effect. And the resident thief—who stole time from those who had run out of time, who stole time to waste time, because otherwise the time would crawl—spent the evening setting each of these watches so that they were synchronous with the watch he had filched from the casket of a childhood lover. In the maddening allegory he was playing out, Repulsion and Compulsion met in the same room, exchanged business cards, and discovered they were twins who had been separated at birth.

The Orrin Effect.

With a loud cry, Sam came into his wife's mouth, and the hotel woke with a single jolt, thinking she had finally killed him. She spit into his face and wiped her chin on his shirt.

Sleep drew them all in. Except for a few. Except specifically for those

who desired it the most, such as Charles Orrin, who labored in a written world that lagged a full ten years behind the life he was living. He
had no hope of closing the gap before he died, so frequently, to dispel
the ghosts that lodged with him and to reassure himself that he still had
a life to live, he would put aside his memoir to write in his journal,
which he did tonight.

"A very important event today," he wrote. "Today a smart young
man, a genius in his own right, came to me, asking me to be his men-
tor. I believe this marks the long-awaited turn. For without disciples,
how will I manage to outlive myself? He will no doubt grow to detest
me, and when this happens, my teaching of the Orrin Effect will be
complete."

❀   ❀   ❀

First thing in the morning, Jerry got up and went down to the café, asking the cook if he could have a job. Immediately, the cook went into the
kitchen and fired the dishwasher, who fell to his knees to give thanks for
his deliverance. At nine o'clock, Dr. Orrin came in and, seeing that Jerry
was working hard, felt unbearably sad and alone. Jerry smiled at him
every time he came out to clear tables, and Dr. Orrin felt that Jerry's
industry was a personal slight. Rachel came through the café, but since
she did not have a planned rendezvous with Lorenzo, she never stopped
to talk to the doctor. The Vietnamese couple came in, but the privacy of
their language offended Dr. Orrin and made him think they were rude.
Finally Franz Meekham came in, without his bulldog.

"Ah, the good reverend," Dr. Orrin called out. "Come and sit with me.
I have a point of theology that I want to discuss with you." With a sour
look on his face, Reverend Meekham took a seat next to Dr. Orrin. "Tell
me, Reverend. I want to understand a small factor of God's purpose. Why
is it that God made old people so ugly and young people so beautiful?"

"Simple," the reverend said. "It's so old people turn away from the
flesh. It's so the young will reject them, and they will repel each other.
Then they can turn to God."

"Oh," the doctor said. He was disappointed with the answer. Of
course, it would have to be simple. Unlike Lawsonomy, Christianity was
a philosophy for simpletons, hence its great success. The minister went
back into the hotel to get his dog Theo for their morning walk, so Dr.
Orrin just sat there, empty and alone once more, until he saw the criminal sneaking through on his way to the street. "Ah, Mr. La Boe!" Dr.
Orrin called out.

The criminal paused in mid-stride and looked at Dr. Orrin from the
corner of his eye. The name he used to register at the hotel was only

vaguely familiar to him, but he knew he had to acknowledge it.

"Yeah? Whadya want?"

"Do you have a spare moment?"

"What do you mean by that, old man?"

"If you've got the time, I'd like to speak to you."

"I'm busy," he said, and he walked away.

"I'm sure you are," Dr. Orrin said, with notable sarcasm. "I'm sure that you just don't have the time."

The criminal tried to ignore this remark. He had almost made his escape when the hand of compulsion overtook him, and he turned back. What did this old man know?

"Sit down, sit down, my friend, and we shall talk." Dr. Orrin patted the stool next to him and the criminal sat down. "This is your parole," Dr. Orrin said. The criminal flinched. "Which is to say a talk, my friend. Just a talk. I couldn't help but notice how you responded to my attitude about the more irrational aspects of time. Perhaps you are a fellow antichronologist?"

"Could be," the criminal said, narrowing his eyes. "What of it?"

"Well, it's just that my studies have been broad and may overlap some of your own. Let us compare notes, shall we? I've found, as I'm sure you're aware, that some of the greatest foibles of humankind have come through their attempt to impose a predetermined infrastructure upon that most ghostly of forces, time. Take the Romans. So in love with the number ten they were, that they assumed there could be no more than ten months. And as bureaucrats, they loved round numbers. Therefore, they decreed that all months would thenceforth be thirty days in length. A simple calculation renders a year as three hundred days.[2] Needless to say, chaos reigned in a few short years, the winter solstice being celebrated as the olives grew ripe and dropped to the ground, unpicked as it were, because it was not time to pick the olives."

"What're ya getting at?"

"Merely a general critique of the outmoded notions of time that we bear with us. Such as the seven-day week! It infuriates me! Only once a year does it divide evenly into the month—and in a leap year not at all! I ask you, Why? Merely because tradition calls the number seven holy?" Dr. Orrin leaned closer to the criminal and whispered loudly. "The Deists are trying to drive us all crazy, all because of their insistence that Time is Spirit! And because of a pathological fear of fractions! As a fellow chronologist, you must share my outrage."

2. Dr. Orrin errs here. The correct number of Roman days in a year, before the adjustments of the Julian calendar, was 304. —The editor.

Indeed, the criminal did. As he listened to the doctor's words, he grew furious. "But . . . what can we do about it?" the criminal asked after a dumbfounded silence, his voice quivering.

"Very little, my friend, short of taking up arms. It took a revolution before the Russians could free themselves from the vagaries of the Eastern calendar. Even so, their calendars were so much in error that what they called the October Revolution actually took place in November!"

The criminal closed his eyes as they teared over in absolute fury at the senselessness of this.

"And so you ask me, what can we do? Well, there's no sense in revising the calendar, adding a day, striking a minute, as the English did, in 1752, when the day after September 2nd became September 14th!"

"The idiots!" the criminal said in a low voice.

"Yes, and not one of these fools have ever noticed what is clear to the most common man, that time speeds up as you age. Do our clocks and calendars account for this?" Dr. Orrin gave a pause. "You have noticed this, haven't you?"

"Why, . . . yes!" the criminal said, taking a deep breath. It was as though he were witnessing for the first time the breadth of a general conspiracy.

"All we can do is to start over! Destroy the clocks! Burn the calendars! The next year shall be the year zero! Need I say more?" Dr. Orrin asked.

"No!" the criminal said, standing. "I see it clearly now!" Taking a smart step back, the criminal saluted the doctor. "I shall always treasure this conversation." Then he turned on his heels, and went out of the restaurant into the street with a renewed sense of mission.

Dr. Orrin was a little surprised by the criminal's furor, but he could not let that alter his plans. After finishing his breakfast, the doctor went out to the front desk and, by his usual technique, drove the concierge from his post. Then the doctor secured the passkey for 105. He went upstairs and let himself into the criminal's room. There he took up the sack of stolen watches that he had discovered the day before. For a moment, it almost seemed they were ticking in unison, but this perfect rhythm quickly decayed and scattered. "Ah," the doctor said to himself. "The poor thief is too Christlike in his methods. He wants to unburden humanity from their sins by taking them all upon himself. But he is not strong enough. I must free him from his current compulsion. I must take him to the next stage."

The doctor gathered up the analog watches, the digital watches, the children's watches with their bright bands, the heirlooms like a family sickness passed on to another generation. He took them out of the hotel, dropping them in a dumpster five blocks away. Night descended without his notice. Suddenly tired, he closed his eyes for a second, and when he opened them red light was leaking around the gray, filthy buildings. The sun seemed to cross the sky at a lower angle, raking the buildings. His shadow, vibrating a little, began to climb the walls.

At that moment, in another time zone, a woman stepped out onto her porch. Suddenly, she understood where her life had gone wrong. She could see, with pitiless clarity, that all the grief she had given to her son was because she was afraid he'd turn out like his father. Now, however, she understood that the very act of directing him away from his father-line had forced him into it. She was an asthmatic to begin with, and the realization took her breath away. She stepped out of the front door of her house for a swallow of night air, when suddenly her skin began to crawl. The neighborhood vibrated. The streetlights blinked out. Coming back to her senses, she found herself on a bus, one hundred miles away, as the driver announced their arrival in a city she had never once visited. Here she was, getting off the bus, wandering a street lined by skull-shaped parking meters, wondering how to begin her search.

Lorenzo Rafi stretched out in his bed, enjoying the sound of Rachel screaming at her husband, when he noticed the lights and the shadows beginning to vibrate. Rachel also noticed the vibrations and briefly paused in her assault. She'd been periodically spitting in Samuel's face, and Samuel sat there, taking it. He didn't even bother to wipe the spittle away. It gathered and hung loosely on his chin while he looked around the room, trying to calculate the cause of the flickering lights. The change seemed subtle, almost lost among the dust motes drifting and the smell of cold cabbage. More obvious to Rachel was the change in Samuel himself, now rising from the chair with his jaws clenched.

Days later, confiding all this to Dr. Orrin, Rachel asserted that all along she had only wanted to get a response from Samuel. She never flagged from maintaining the claim that all her abuse of him was just to unleash the strong man who, she was certain, lived inside Samuel's dough-colored exterior. If so, then that night was to bring about the completion of her desire, for suddenly Samuel grabbed her with arms that had grown strong from years of kneading dough, and he shoved her into the hall. That was the extent of his violence, but that alone, Rachel said, was devastating.

With utter horror, Reverend Meekham watched his bulldog drop a litter of puppies on the floor. With equal horror, Lorenzo Rafi felt a single tear swell up in his eye. He wiped it away and examined it, intrigued, as if it were a mysterious piece of filth. The concierge went down into the bowels of the hotel in order to find the cause of the unexplained vibrations and the flickering lights, when he lost his balance, falling down a flight of stairs, unaccountably laughing about this as if it were a great thrill. Hearing all these sounds, Jerry Hauser crept into the hall. The hotel was entirely dark and populated by barking dogs and screaming people. When the lights came back, he returned to practicing his guitar, momentarily confused because he didn't remember buying it.

It was as if the entire hotel had found a single mind, which turned its astonished attention to the third floor, where Rachel banged on the door of her room, begging Samuel, "Oh, please, Samuel! I'll try to do better! I'll—I'll do nice things for you! I'll cook you cabbage and wash your clothes and never, never have a harsh thing to say. . . . Samuel? If you don't let me sleep with you, why I'll have to sleep with someone else. I'm warning you! I'll—I'll sleep with Larry!"

Hearing his name, Lorenzo bolted from his bed and pressed his ear against the door.

"Oh, yes. I will! And I want you to know that I've been sleeping with him for—for years! He satisfies me! He doesn't grope around! He knows where to touch me!"

Lorenzo jumped into bed and hid under his blankets, terrified, and a moment later Rachel was at his door. "Let me in, Larry! I can't stand it anymore!" For a while, he tried to ignore her but she wouldn't give up, so he let her in, if only to shut her up. Immediately she attacked him, pushing him backward to his bed, ripping off his robe, forcing her body against him. But this forward moving, tumbling, sprawling action came to a sudden halt when she discovered that Larry was unaccountably flaccid. Indeed, he wept in shame at this fact, because at that very moment, contrary to his wishes, even against the soul of his very character, he started to feel as if he loved her. Not only that, but he told her so.

It was a humiliating discovery for both of them, perhaps for Rachel even more than for Larry. She wept as well, and cursed at him, and claimed that he was using his love for her as an excuse to get out of making love to her. "Oh!" she yelled, taking a punch at his face, "you don't want me either!" But that was simply not the case. The way Larry explained it to Dr. Orrin, his sudden impotence was merely the result of his discomfort with this strange new emotion, this weird tenderness he felt as he stroked her hair, murmuring comforting words that seemed completely foreign to his mouth.

The next day Larry never left his room for fear of meeting the wronged husband. He remained in bed, slipping in and out of sleep, dreaming of Samuel who appeared before him, strong and erect, with a bull's golden horns on his head. "Ah," Dr. Orrin said when he heard the dream. "Those are the horns that you yourself put there, but now they are the symbol of Samuel's authority!" Unfortunately, Lorenzo could not understand what the doctor meant by this. And so days passed. Finally famished, Lorenzo ventured to the dirty café that he always considered beneath his elevated tastes, and there was Samuel, staring into a black cup of coffee, as if it harbored the blackest deed that he would ever commit. Lorenzo would have escaped the café on the spot, but he was convinced that showing his fear would provoke the man, so instead he tried to appear dispassionate as he took a seat, expecting the outraged husband to attack him at any moment. His hands trembled violently. He scalded his tongue on his first sip of coffee. He almost choked, feeling a strong hand patting him on the shoulder.

"Don't take it, friend," Sam said to him. "The poor woman hates herself, but she'll take it out on you."

Sam walked into the street as Larry Rafi humiliated himself further by bawling in the sight of everyone. Jerry Hauser and the cook watched from the kitchen, feeling nothing but disgust, as a woman paused at the window where she taped a photocopy of a young boy's face. She wore a scarf and sunglasses as if she didn't want to be recognized.

❀   ❀   ❀

That evening, Dr. Orrin was surprised to be visited by no fewer than a half dozen people, including Samuel and Rafi and finally Rachel. They all wanted advice—and they all, unaccountably, were a great annoyance to the doctor, who in the past would have been gratified to have so many people seeking out his wisdom. Even the concierge came to him, surprised by the explosion of traffic in the lobby. There was a finer style of clothing in the hotel these days, a quieter clientele, and there were more prestigious addresses in his register, so he watched the doctor with attentive eyes as the doctor explained that the hotel was getting the general reputation as a place to go, not to hide, but to heal. Once it stood as an outward manifestation of the shame of its clients. "Now," the doctor said, taking off his spectacles and rubbing away a spot, "the hotel seems to take their shame away. You have a gold mine here, my man, so do take care to exploit it."

But despite the confidence with which he handed out advice, the doctor was deeply uneasy. He had the pronounced sense that his life was starting over, that he was a buoyant child taking his first dip in the ocean. In his journal he wrote: "Something very profound has happened. It might stand to reason that a deeply sublime change, something akin to the birth of a deity, or the injection of the spirit by means of force into the course of human history—something like this might result in the unnerving changes I have noticed about me."

But he continued to wonder what had happened. What accounted for the missing days and the switched polarities in the human temperament? At night, he sometimes heard the Reverend Meekham uttering passionate blasphemies. By day, he heard the more than proficient sound of skittering guitar strings coming through his walls. And then one day he thought of it.

"How foolish of me! I, of all people, should have understood. After all, the phenomenon was named after me! I am the eyes and ears of the hotel. I am the sentient power that makes the building human. I am the hotel's flickering consciousness! But, oh, the injustice of it! Now I will receive all the attention that I ever desired, but because of the effect I will be ungrateful. I will want to be alone!" He skipped two lines and wrote in bold letters, "The Orrin Effect!" and he closed his journal for the last time. It was a profound tragedy. Once, he desired many things—beauty, attention, respect—but now . . . But now he realized with a shudder that he would be desired! And, for the first time in his long life, he despaired.

"Doctor? Are you in? Please, doctor, can I see you for a second? I have a new song I want you to hear."

"I'm working," the doctor shouted.

"This is one I wrote myself," the boy said.

Dr. Orrin let the boy in and slumped into a chair. The boy tuned his guitar and started to play a fairly listenable refrain, repetitious but melodic enough since he only used one chord, and then he started to sing:

> I don't knooow what I waaaant,
> yippy-kai-yo-kai-yo-kai-yay!
> I don't knooow what I waaaant,
> yippy-kai-yo-kai-yo-kai-yay!

"Enough!" the doctor cried.

"Well I don't know where to take it from there," the boy said, sounding defensive.

"Take it back to your room!" the doctor said, so the boy did. The doctor sat there, dismayed, disgusted. After holding his face in his hands for a solid five minutes, he went back to his work. He was no longer working on his memoirs. He would never work on them again, he knew this for certain, and he would never again attempt to explain the ways of Lawson to Man. He dreaded to think what would happen to the General Theory once it was broadly accepted—as now he knew it would be. Acceptance would prove his theory wrong, wouldn't it? So what he had in mind now was a smaller project, the achievement of an unparalleled fame through the act of insulting as many morons as he could by means of a small, overpriced pamphlet. Its working title would be

ADAGES FOR STINKING ANIMALS

1. Publication is the quickest path to obscurity. If I make myself known to you all, it is in the hopes that you will grow tired of me and give me back my solitude. . . .

54. If you want kindness, be cruel. If you want love, act indifferent. Shun everyone whom you would want to know. . . .

66. Don't believe in Jesus until he believes in you. . . .

103. Be bitter while you are young, for when you are old you will be too tired. . . .

❀　　❀　　❀

The boy, although he was only sixteen, was sick to death. Try as he might, he could not write a song, he hated his music, and because he hated it, he could think of nothing else. Just that day, he had gone out looking for the banjo player—the street musician—whom he now blamed for setting him down this dreaded path. He planned to kill the bum. Eventually he would, but today he could not find him.

After working in the kitchen all day, Jerry was on his way through the lobby when he saw that a woman was talking to Dr. Orrin. She was asking the doctor if he knew a Jerry Hauser, and the doctor said yes. Hearing this, Jerry grabbed a newspaper to cover his face, and he slumped down into a lounge chair.

"Yes? You know him?" the woman said hopefully. "Do you expect to see him again?"

"Yes," the doctor said. The woman started weeping for joy. "But actually that is a lie," the doctor said. "Let me explain. By saying yes, I am attempting to avoid the possibility that I will ever know him." The woman stared at him, baffled. "It's a superstition I have. Things never turn out in the way you'd expect, so my philosophy—my talisman—is to expect the worst. Meeting your son, Madam, if he's anything like you, would certainly qualify under that baleful category."

She looked at him. She couldn't understand why this old man, this stranger, would try to be so cruel. Yet for some reason, she was unbearably attracted to him. She looked him over. It could not be the old man's sagging frame or his pipe-fouled breath. It must be his resolute sense of himself. Yes, that was it. Here was a man who knew who he was. The woman excused herself from Dr. Orrin's presence and went off to find a pay phone so she could call her husband and tell him she wanted a divorce, and Jerry used the opportunity to escape back to his room.

He hated his room now, and therefore it seemed just like home. He spent as much time in his room as he could, and he could not help but feel a shudder of dread as he opened the door to see his guitar waiting for him, its mouth open as if it wanted to be fed. This begging, hungry expression angered Jerry, especially tonight as he felt his mother's presence in the hotel, attempting to track him down. He picked up a bottle of soda pop, still sealed but now warm, and he was just about to jam the bottle down the guitar's throat when the bottle slipped from his hands, its contents spraying over everything, his bedspread, the walls.

The old wallpaper went transparent. Slowly, words appeared, whole lines, complete stanzas. It took him only a moment to recognize that this was the poetry of Polanski bleeding through. Dr. Orrin had told him once that just when the poet ran out of paper, his creativity took off. The walls became his pages. As Jerry read the words, chords and melody came to him, immediately and without effort. He didn't want the music to come. He was already tired of it. He took more pleasure in washing dishes. But the music came anyway. It was a painful, brutal thing to happen, and Jerry resented it. But he had no choice. He turned to his guitar, still sticky from soda pop, its mouth still open, and he started to play while the walls spoke to him. Even more disturbing was the fact that the poet's words fit perfectly into his own mouth, where he briefly shaped them, and they were his own. Jerry felt the bitter theft you feel when you discover that your favorite complaints are voiced by nearly everyone.

Later that night, the Reverend Meekham, uttering blasphemies, shoved Jerry's mother back into the hall. She was going door to door asking everyone if they knew her son, and suddenly she thought of that beautiful, rude old man she'd met in the lobby. At that very moment, Dr. Orrin—who did not suspect that the woman was creeping up to his door—was in a deep dream. He was dreaming that he went door to door, selling vacuum cleaners. In the walls of the hotel, the crickets tisked. The radiators started to clack and shoot out steam. Just down the hall, Rachel made love to Samuel, who couldn't care less. In the dark, by himself, Larry Rafi listened to them and sobbed.

While Jerry Hauser sang a melodic song, made out of the words of a poet whose talents were thin, his mother paused at Dr. Orrin's door. Not recognizing the sound of her lost son's voice, she started to tap her feet. She wished that her son would play music like that, but she knew that he wouldn't even know a person so gifted, much less be that gifted. She was so convinced of this that she didn't bother to knock on her son's door even after Dr. Orrin shoved her back into the hall, where she stood, eyes closed, next to tears, listening to the sound of the guitar, which seemed to recede as though it were moving far away from her.

That night, the hotel's residents sank into a sleep so deep that you might suppose they would not wake up for anything, not even for a fire, with smoke-filled rooms no different from the heavy medium of their sleep. But on a night not so very far into the future, nearly every resident would come suddenly awake, feeling alive as never before, the sirens going off all over the town. The elephant's trunk of a tornado would be moving down the street, sucking up shingles and cinders, neon lights and gutter trash, and one or two of the town's sleeping citizens. Sam would carry the now emaciated form of Larry down into the basement, followed by the Reverend Meekham and his pack of yapping bulldogs, tumbling down the steps past a slow-moving Rachel, her hand on the rail, leaning back against the counterweight of her pregnancy. Jerry would be there waiting for them, imagining how they had all fallen into his trap. For days he'd been trying to find a pawnshop willing to trade his guitar for a gun.

The last to stumble down into the basement would be the concierge, clutching the hotel's registry, his life story and his legacy, and when all of them had gathered there, huddling in a room full of crusted pipes, they would take stock of their numbers and realize the doctor wasn't with them. A toilet would flush, the old pipes gurgling, as they'd realize Doctor Orrin was still in his room. He would be moving with difficulty toward his sloped-backed bed, staring up as the winds opened up a new skylight, his table lamp exploding, his disparate writings swirling around him as the gullet of the storm moved directly overhead, and he would ascend, weeping, joyous, justified.

That singular night would come, a certainty so great that Dr. Orrin had already recorded it in his book. But on the night that Jerry Hauser's mother stood weeping outside his room, nothing extraordinary happened. The hotel was merely full of the usual pilgrims and escapees and unprepared retirees. There was no room for Jerry's mother when she applied at the desk, so she went out, still searching, into the dangerous night. A man began to follow her, keeping to the shadows. He had a watch in his pocket, and he meant to give it to her. He had no idea why he wanted to do this. The face of the watch glowed in the dark, but its arms did not move. He considered it to be a thing of great beauty, like a desecrated corpse. As she crossed the street, unwittingly moving into a street of dark alleys and warehouses and trash, she saw him hunch over, hurrying after her. She might have been afraid, but there was a new song playing in her head that night. An infectious melody, it comforted her as she walked—and as the man ducked ahead of her, waiting in the dark to give her his gift, her own watch found the rhythm and this song stayed with her. So long as she could hear it, she knew that she was safe.

Tales of the Yodeling Radio Waves

"THE YODEL IS a strange art," Happy said, warming to the subject. He poured us both an aquavit and seemed impressed when I downed it without lifting my pencil from the page. "Over the years I've made quite a study of it, and let me tell you first off that the Swiss of the Alps and the Pygmies of Africa are the best damn yodelers in the known world! Not that I've ever heard a Pygmy yodel. I have that on the authority of the *World Book Encyclopedia,* but I always thought that it would really be something else. I'd have to say that it's one of the big disappointments of my life that I never did."

I wrote that down.

"Anyhow, no matter how much I studied the yodel—and I studied it like a man whose life depended on it because it did—the yodel always remained a mystery, you know. There was that sex part to it. Something about sex, I knew that. Mind you, I didn't want to tell Yolanda about that part. She's always been an old-fashioned girl. I figured that it would just make her self-conscious. But I was older than she was. I'd been around. And I knew it was partly sex. But it was something more than that, too. Partly it was the way Yolanda would seem to go into a trance when she yodeled. She'd stop being who she was, as if she were the vessel for some greater force. Sometimes the sound of the yodel seemed so strange that I figured God was yodeling right through Yolanda's body. Because the yodel does things to people, you know. I once saw a man go into a fit, right there in the audience. I've seen people black out, and when they woke up they said they'd talked to their long-dead kin. People'd say they could hear Yolanda from miles away, and their dogs would stop barking and sit quiet, listening, like they hoped to learn something."

I wrote all this down.

"We got our first steady job on radio with a certain Reverend Doctor

Ishmael Baker, who claimed to be able to cure impotence and cancer. The Yodelaires were just a musical interlude, or at least that's what our contract read, but folks said that if anyone was healed, it was Yolanda's music that did it. Folks said that after the Reverend was gunned down by some distraught man in Iowa City, Yolanda went on yodeling, and people went on healing.

"Since radio was such a boost to our careers, I figured I should make a study of it. I had an engineer explain to me what the radio waves were, and when I couldn't understand that, I had him draw me a picture of one, and then I said to myself, 'Well, now. This makes sense.' I always figured that the troughs and peaks of the radio wave just matched the valleys and hilltops of Yolanda's voice. I figured that the art of the yodel would start to bloom in the radio age, like they were made for each other, and that's pretty much what happened.

"Then the Federal Radio Commission sent us a warning that we were under suspicion of going beyond our power limits. Of course we hadn't— and I wrote them right back and told them that. I said that it was just that the radio wave and the yodel reinforced each other, and together they were at least five times more powerful than each of them alone, and I had the figures to prove it. I did, too."

❀   ❀   ❀

All said, the war had been a fantastic experience for them. They'd written special yodeling war anthems: "The War Yodel," "Yankee Doodle Yodel," "Yokohama Yodel," "Yodeling on the Rhine," on and on. Band members contributed racy lyrics, but Yolanda much preferred to do her sentimental hit "I'm Longing Just to Hold You Again and Yodel in Your Arms." Years later, as Happy recounted this to me, reclining in his comfortable and well-stocked library, he assumed a serious tone as he said, "But I want you to know that I was profoundly affected by the fact that our troops would go off to kill and be killed after Yolanda yodeled for them. Singing for those guys was more than just a career move. Sometimes it seemed like Yolanda was kissing them good-bye. But I'd be less than honest if I didn't admit that, at the same time, I couldn't help but think how we were going to be famous after the war was over. You can imagine how let down we felt when we got back stateside and folks weren't so much interested in yodeling anymore. I didn't know why. Maybe they wanted bands as big as platoons. Maybe they wanted music you could dance to, so you could lean against that long-lost love. Anyway, yodeling was out, and it was that quick. We still had our station in Muscatine, Iowa, though. We still had county fairs and harvest festivals across the Midwest. We'd even yodel on the rodeo circuit. . . ."

It had been a hard truth to take, a truth that had been disguised during the war years by their furious receptions and frenzied audiences throughout the European Theater and even the Far East. During the war, they'd once heard Yolanda's yodel echoing out of an Oriental radio. They'd heard Yolanda yodel on a radio that cruised the Indian Ocean, but that was all past.

Happy once dreamed that Yolanda would be asked to yodel the national anthem at Wrigley Field. He dreamed that she would yodel Wagner in Carnegie Hall. Even though none of that ever happened, Happy sometimes thought that it still could, because with every passing year, Yolanda seemed to get better and better at her art. And then there were other times, when Happy was depressed and bewildered by the rapidity of their rise and fall. Since he was used to dealing with the public, he knew that there were forces larger than talent alone that controlled their popularity. He thought that maybe these forces were even larger than the public, a grand scale of temperatures, tides, fads and fashions, a gigantic pattern of a sweeping rise and fall.

At times like this he felt that the yodel was the victim of its own universal signature; however, on a smaller scale, Happy sometimes blamed the decline of the yodel on the rise of country music in general—"and Patsy Montana in particular," he said. He tracked her career. It climbed up as Yolanda's declined. He half considered a lawsuit. But then he thought that maybe Patsy had the right idea. She was taking the yodel to something else. She wasn't afraid of crossing boundaries. She did whatever she could to stay at the top. She was no purist. She wasn't even from Montana, which galled Happy, quite a bit, sometimes.

Happy constantly surprised me. One night, as we sat up late, we had a fairly learned discussion of how the yodel was like the other arts, how the yodel shared with all the arts the same pattern of swelling popularity and then diminishing influence. Happy admitted to me that in his darker moments he half considered the possibility that—like tapestry—yodeling was a dead art. I marveled at his knowledge until I considered the fact that, with their fall in popularity, their bookings were few and their hours of leisure long. Happy explained to me that when an art starts to die, it begins to look inward, monitoring its life signs, becoming self-conscious. "People're no different," he said. "When they start to grow old, they start talking about themselves, their aches and pains, way too much." Yolanda's last hit was entitled "The Yodeling Song," but that could have been the name for the last ten songs she wrote. They always went like this—

"When I was a little girl my daddy sat me on his knee and taught me how to yodel and it went like this—"

And then she'd start to yodel.

"You see," Happy said, "yodeling doesn't use words and such. And so there's a real problem in it, in that you can't yodel about something like a broken heart or being drunk. Oh sure, you could sing a song about a broken-hearted drunken yodeler, but it always comes to one thing. You start out by singing something like—

"'I met a broken-hearted sad old man who was always drunk and he said he used to yodel and it always went like this—'

"And then you *have* to yodel. And it always comes down to that, the yodel. Because anything you might add to the yodel is just going to be another silly introduction, just another excuse to yodel one more time. . . ."

After their fifth year of bad bookings, in a desperate state of mind, Happy began to press for drastic changes. He pressured Yolanda to go against her nature and her talent. He wanted her to experiment. Later he regretted it, because he was sure it was this that led to Yolanda's medical problem. He had plenty of time to regret his experiments in the years that followed, years in which they had nothing but time and each other. When Happy grew old, he often said that the only children they had were their memories. He tried to disown his regrets, but he couldn't. He wished he had been content with their aging audience. He wished that he would have been at ease with the fact that even their biggest fans really only wanted to listen to yodeling part of the time.

"We probably would have been better off if Yolanda hadn't been the best," Happy confided. "I mean the acknowledged best, the queen of the yodel. Everyone said so. No one ever contested it. She didn't even have a close runner-up. Even Patsy Montana thought so. I'll tell you straight out that I once heard Patsy say, 'Yolanda Larson is the finest darn yodeler in the *world*.' Of course, Patsy Montana *had* to sing country, because she really couldn't yodel for squat. At least not for more than four bars. But Yolanda could yodel until the cows came home, which was of course its original purpose, and so she kinda had to, because nobody else could. And now I want you to write something down. I want it put exactly as I'm putting now. It's important. Are you ready?"

I was always ready to write.

"There is not a greater curse," Happy said distinctly, "than being the best, the undisputed best there is, at a dying art. Got that?"

"Do you want the book to start that way?" I asked.

"Oh God, no. God. No, you'd better bury that deep inside a final chapter some place. It's too dark a thought for a beginning. Who'd start anything, if they knew it was just going to come to that?"

⊛   ⊛   ⊛

I never had the chance to interview Yolanda. She was a white-haired ghost who wandered through the house and smiled at me sometimes. Happy told me that he met her just when Jimmie Rodgers was inventing country music, stealing the yodel away from the Swiss traditionalists for good. But as Happy always said, "There was room for a purist in those days." And a pedigreed yodeler she was, descended from an unbroken chain of yodelers that went back to a time when the Alps were the only thing that stuck out of the ice.

"When I first heard the sound," Happy said, "I could hardly believe my ears. So I drove around the countryside and searched and squinted and hunted around, and that sound seemed like it was coming from, oh, the trees, the grass. Everywhere. And I can't even tell you what it sounded like, because it sounded, well . . . like angels up in snowy heaven. Like sunlight bouncing off a winter lake.

"I looked for days before I finally discovered her tending the cows. It was her daddy that taught her to yodel, and it was her daddy's decision whether or not she would travel with my band. And the only reason he let her go was because he knew for sure that Yolanda could take the yodel places it had never gone before. So we signed the contracts and then I rode that crest. That's how Yolanda Larson and the Yodelaires were born. I just strapped on my accordion and after that I made Yolanda's fortune my fortune, the highs and lows, whatever." Which is not to say that Happy didn't think of giving it up. He did, and ever more frequently as the years passed. But then, just as the slump in their popularity was starting to look permanent, Yolanda's daddy died, of throat cancer, no less. And when his dying word was nothing less than a wavy line on a piece of paper, Yolanda was in tears: "I will, Daddy, I won't ever stop, I won't let you down."

"Well, that cinched it," Happy said. After that Yolanda was determined to keep singing, not for fame or fortune, but just to make sure that the yodel got passed on. She might have even been content just to pass the gift on to her children, but that hadn't happened. "Oh, we tried," Happy said. "God knows we tried." In fact, there was one year that they worked at having children every chance they got. Happy took Yolanda on a vacation in northern Minnesota. They were out in a boat, the water softly lapping the shore, their boat rising and falling and rocking on the waves. And for some reason, Happy begged her to yodel for him. She did. He was entranced. Then he coaxed her to take off her clothes, and so she did, and he did, too. Then he put his face against her belly and begged, again, for her to yodel. She did. He laughed like a child. Things progressed to this and that, the boat, the waves, the rocking, the yodel—and when Yolanda looked up, a large band of loons had gathered around them, their red eyes open, as if they were scared, as if they were drawn to her sound against their will.

"Happy?" she asked.

She loved his name, and so she said it again. He struggled awake with a start, confused by their location, the bright light and shadows wavering on the surface of the lake.

"Look!" Yolanda said, but her plain, urgent voice had broken the loons' trance. With a single motion, they dipped under the water, and after that, her bright-eyed children did not come any closer. From then on, Yolanda realized that if the yodel were going to outlive her, if she were going to honor the memory of her daddy, then she would just have to pass the gift on to the world of strangers. "And that meant a comeback of some kind," Happy said. And so toward this end, Happy brooded, he studied, and sometimes he drank. "A bit too much in those days," he said, pouring me another aquavit.

It was the age of big bands. At first Happy half considered adding a few dozen musicians and taking the yodel in the direction that Lawrence Welk had taken the polka. But then there came a day when he was in a club in Chicago, and he heard a bebop band going full tilt, and he thought to himself: "My God, this is it! If Patsy and Jimmie Rodgers can take the yodel down one path, down the country path, Yolanda and I can take it down the other. The better path. Because this is the only path that can leave the words behind if it wants to. Imagine that. Jazz. No words!"

Words had always gotten in the way of the yodel anyway, so he started taking her to jazz clubs in Chicago, a fair drive from their radio station in Muscatine. On their first night out, Yolanda said the music made her dizzy, and Happy said, "Don't listen to it. Just feel it. Find the rhythms. Get inside the key signatures." Yolanda closed her eyes and hiccuped. They had to leave early. The second night, it wasn't much better. Happy made her take deep breaths, but he wasn't going to give up. He told himself that nothing was ever born without labor and pain, and he told her that, too. And Yolanda, with Happy right next to her, was doing nothing less than giving birth to a brand new art form.

Although Happy was convinced that somehow this was the direction that their music should go, he knew he had to be careful. To fire the Yodelaires at this point would be foolish, so Happy had no choice but to sink their life savings into hiring a new band, at least for weekends. And at first it all seemed hopeful. During the first session, one of the musicians brought a friend to sit in on the tenor sax, and Happy was surprised to see how small this saxophonist was. He was incredibly small. Happy hired him on the spot. For a while Happy just had Yolanda follow the lead of the small black man on tenor sax, hoping for some intercontinental spark to flash. He hoped that the yodel would come back to life with an infusion of African music, as so many other important forms of music had. Happy said that you couldn't find a better teacher than this man, who taught without speaking, who thought that words just got in the way. Yolanda understood, and she relaxed into the music more quickly than everyone expected, and everything looked extremely hopeful indeed. She even sang scat, and the musicians—tough judges all—pronounced her scat-singing passable, even good, considering that she carried her whole life the vague hint of a Teutonic accent.

This experiment was, however, short-lived. Just as soon as Yolanda kicked in with her full-voiced yodel, the mood of the music altered horribly. It was like a large-scale car pileup on the highway—horns blaring, brakes squealing, random thumps, random crashes. The musicians all stopped and stared at the floor like someone had died. No one had to say anything. Happy paid them off, and they went on their way, shaking their heads, trying not to laugh. But even so, Happy really enjoyed the experiment. At the time, he didn't regret trying it. He'd learned a lot. He even had the sense to realize that there was probably a funny story there, buried in his own disappointment. He hoped that the musicians got a laugh out of the experience. It might even be one they would tell to their children and grandchildren, and he was glad for that.

For her own part, Yolanda was relieved when the experiment was over. On the way back to Muscatine, she sang in German and yodeled to herself, while Happy went deep inside himself. Yolanda always seemed vulnerable, always a little birdlike when she sang, and as the car surged forward and her small voice undulated against the flat baseline of the fields outside Chicago, Happy had thought to himself: "Better to be completely unknown, than to be a bad joke, a famous old joke. I could never let that happen to Yolanda." Happy gave a thoughtful pause before he said to me, "And, speaking off the record, if Lawrence Welk doesn't watch it, he might become an old joke, too!" I didn't have the heart to tell him that this had already happened.

❀   ❀   ❀

After the untimely death of the bebop yodel, Happy and Yolanda were still relatively young. They had lives to live, so they went back on the air, with renewed commitment and no illusions. They accepted whatever would come, even if they would become the shadows of an old, outmoded tradition. One day, they were in the studio, trying to record a jingle for Swiss Miss. "Or maybe it was Wisconsin cheese," Happy said. In later years, he couldn't remember. "Anyway," he said, "it was a big contract, more important than it might have been in the past since I'd taken such a big soaking in that bebop thing."

A company representative attended their recording session, and their most able Yodelaires were there as well: Happy himself was on accordion, Ralph "The Rooster" Schmidt was on clarinet, and Ernst Meyer was on tuba. Even a few of Yolanda and Happy's closest friends, aware of the importance of this contract, were hanging about the studio to give them support. Their preparations for this day had been tireless, their rehearsals tense. Happy hoped that the best of their musicians and all of their talents would come together to produce one last jingle, do or die. Happy himself was to going to come in at the end of the jingle and do the sales pitch. He trusted no one else to do it right.

Still every bit a perfectionist, Happy had the band run through the jingle a couple times for the company rep, who sat quietly for a while before he said: "Rhythm. It needs more rhythm." They brought in their banjo player and their drummer, and ran through the one-minute jingle another time, and the company rep said, "A richer sound. A bigger sound, please." They brought in a Hawaiian guitar. But that wasn't enough. The company rep said, "Good. Very good. But play it . . . faster!" And on the second time through the song, something terrible happened. Yolanda started to ululate wildly, warbling out the same two notes until she ran out of air and fell into unconsciousness. At first, Happy thought it was a heart attack, but Yolanda recovered so quickly that Happy decided that she had only hyperventilated.

After a moment's rest, the company rep still insisted on the breakneck speed, so the banjo set the rhythm. Aside from the fact that Yolanda was more tensed than usual, aside from the clear image Happy had of a truck careening down a mountain road with no brakes, the jingle seemed to be coming together. Happy was just about to come in with his sales pitch when he saw Yolanda staring at him, helpless, with the same terrified look in her eyes that people get when they suck a piece of meat down their windpipe.

Happy rushed over to slap her on the back when he heard that she was still yodeling, only now she was out of control. She was yodeling with a voice that seemed to be getting stronger, sucking all her air away. Yolanda waved her arms in front of her face, helpless, as her voice broke another octave higher, higher than Happy had ever heard her sing before. And then she began to yodel in a tight, intricate pattern that seemed like a yodeler's version of speaking in tongues. The musicians stopped playing, dumbfounded, and stared at her. They'd never seen or heard anything like this, either. The sound was unearthly, without quite being heavenly, a warbling cry that seemed to be halfway between a birdsong and the sound of a high-speed machine. And the pattern did not repeat itself. It was like a code that was continually scrambled. With the little control there was left to her, Yolanda tried to cut down the volume so her breath wouldn't leak out all at once. She struggled to shape her voice into a pinhole of song, a teapot sound. Her voice raced up and down the scales like raindrops on a xylophone, and the sound transfixed Happy until he could not tell if he was happy or scared out of his wits. All he could do was watch as her face turned purple, until finally, and maybe even mercifully, Yolanda passed out.

Happy fell to his knees, slumping over her body, and when he felt how cold her skin was, he began to howl and kiss Yolanda's mouth and weep, and the musicians considered how they were going to part him from her, how they were going to pull him away and begin making the dreadful final arrangements. But before long, Yolanda opened her eyes. She saw Happy blubbering over her, and she said, "Dear? Happy sweetie? What's wrong? What's the matter, dear heart?" And hearing her voice, Happy started crying all the harder. Yolanda cried, too. They cried together. And even though terrified, Happy could not help but enjoy the sweet sound they were making, a sound just for the two of them, a cappella, needing no one else. The musicians seemed to know this. They left the room as Happy hugged his dear Yolanda and gave up all ambition, bawling his head off. Maybe, in later years, Happy had his regrets. Maybe he thought that their memories were children that had turned against them. But right then he decided that this was the high point of his life, and he treasured the sweetness of drawing deep breaths and weeping in each other's arms. Happy knew that whatever happened after that would be fine.

❀　　❀　　❀

When Happy glanced over my notes, I could tell that he found pleasure in them. He was cheerful as he gave me the second of four cash payments, the third to come with the completion of the manuscript, the last just before I put the books in his hands. Six months later, our deal was complete. I sent him one thousand copies of *Tales of the Yodeling Radio Waves*, and Yolanda and Happy passed into their private histories. Although the plastic spiral binding of their autobiography reminded Happy of a church cookbook and the reproduction of Happy and Yolanda's favorite photograph of themselves was, at best, primitive, Happy informed me that their friends delighted very much in receiving their own autographed copies at Christmas. Happy even said that there were a few old fans who occasionally wrote letters over time, and for their thoughtfulness they each received a book.

"And by the way," Happy said. "Your proofreading is impeccable."

"Thank you," I said, shifting in my chair with pleasure. It's good to have your work recognized.

Many more years have passed since then. I still hear from them. For me, this was merely another job, but they consider me—as many of my clients do—to be a member of their larger family. In one of his later letters, Happy wrote me that as he and Yolanda grew old together, their lives seemed to get happier every year. He remarked that he sometimes regretted that he had not waited a few more years to write the final chapter: "When I read over our words, I sometimes fear that people will not see our life as the great success and joy that it has been."

This is a common regret among my clients, so I wrote back to Happy immediately and told him what I tell everyone. I said, "If you had waited for the perfect ending, you might not have been alive to read it." Happy wrote back that he saw the sense of my words, and I was glad for that. I always like a satisfied customer. He said that even though the book seemed somehow incomplete, he was content, once again, as he had been so many times before, to resign himself to whatever happened.

And this is what happened: the sun rose and the moon fell once a day for twenty years, and every one of those years I prepared for them their "Christmas Yodeling Newsletter." One day, a number of years later, a little girl heard Yolanda yodeling in the evening as she was calling in the few cows they kept in their retirement. The little girl followed Yolanda home and then charmed her into yodeling. Sitting on the porch, Yolanda sang "The Yodeling Song," and she found that her voice was still strong. More than that, it was unearthly. The sound transfixed the little girl. She wanted to reach into Yolanda's mouth. And the next day the girl brought along her little friends, and in the following years, Yolanda slowly built a choir of full-throated little girls in alpine smocks. They called themselves the Yodeling Heidis and visited rest homes where the old folks cried for half-remembered joy.

As an old woman, Yolanda would step outside at night, even in winter, and sing into the wind, her voice getting better with every passing year. Hearing her, Happy would put down his encyclopedia and turn down the radio and marvel. He would look out the window where the years raced by. The leaves were falling, the snowdrifts rising. They lived in a place where there were hills all around them, a place guarded from the wild ululation of fashion and fame, a place where winter had no echo, where spring was full of warbling music. When the snow melted, they listened as their valley filled back up with sound. The rain came down. The Heidis replenished themselves. And each year when the birds returned, Yolanda and Happy laughed, surprised that chickadees and whip 'o wills would always remember their old songs.

A Bedtime Story

OKAY NOW. This is your story, and I'm only gonna tell one, so no whining when I'm finished. This happened when your mommy was a little girl. We all went out just before Halloween, looking for a good-sized pumpkin to carve up. Out to this farm we heard about. Your mommy had a pretty basket, and she walked around and loaded it up with tiny gourds and squash and blue and white Indian corn. It was autumn, and some of the leaves were hanging in the air, and some were floating down, and some were still on the trees, but they were reaching toward the earth like they could hardly wait to get themselves down and relax, stretch out a bit.

This farm had a load of peacocks, too. Every once in a while one'd come flying out of the barn like he was scared of something in there, and your mommy got scared, too. She came running to me and climbed up in my arms, wanting me to help the bird, but I didn't know what she meant until I heard the peacock calling out, " 'Elp! 'Elp! 'Elp!" so then I knew where she was getting this. That peacock would come running out of the barn, trying to get airborne and yelling "Help!" and "Help!" like he hardly thought he'd get through the day alive. There were these other birds, too, a couple guineas and turkeys and a lot of fancy, stuck-up chickens. And when we were walking around the farmyard, we came up on these geese, which kinda lowered their heads at us and hissed, like they were mean, so I kept your mommy close.

And then I saw a Studebaker Nighthawk! I could hardly believe it. It was up on blocks there, in back of the barn right out there in the open, a beautiful, long low car with just a bubble of a cab. And it had fins, too, just like what I always wanted. I always wanted a car like that. So then this farmer who owned this farm, he came up to me and introduced himself, and I said to him, "So, Kris. You gonna sell me this car?"

And he says, "Nope."

So then I surprised myself by naming flat out a price, a good one, too, but he turned me down and says the reason why he can't sell me the car is because the car belongs to his brother, and his brother is dead. Well, the paint on that Nighthawk had pretty much gone to dust anyway, all blasted away by the sunlight. The thought of that beautiful car out in the open almost made me sick, but I didn't say anything because it wasn't my business. I was afraid that if I said something I'd just get mad. This Kris fellow was pretty quiet, too. But I noticed he was shifting around like he felt guilty about something, and pretty soon he says, "Nope. No, I just can't sell you that Nighthawk. But why don't you go ahead and take your pick of all these pumpkins. You can take all you want. And you can have them for free, too."

Well, I guess he wanted to make it up to us, and that was pretty nice of him, and I told him so, and he just says, "Oh, those pumpkins just grow out in the compost, anyway. I don't even have to coax 'em along."

So your mommy got her pick of all those pumpkins. They were gnarly and twisted-looking and lopsided, almost too scary to carve a face into. They looked like if you stuck a knife into one of them, you just might let something loose, something you really didn't want loose. And your mom, she picked out the homeliest, saddest pumpkins you ever saw, almost like she felt sorry for them, and there was one pumpkin that was homelier than all the rest, and that's the one she wanted to carry around like it was her baby doll. And you know what she told me? She told me she was gonna give that pumpkin a face. Hell, it almost had a face already, or at least the beginnings of one, like it didn't quite get finished with the job of growing a face before it got picked.

Kris hung out with me while I watched your mommy pick out her pumpkins, and for a long time he didn't say anything. And then he walked us to our car like it was some kinda obligation, and he watched us load up the pumpkins. And it looked like he was just gonna stand there and stare at us while we were driving off, when all of a sudden he says, "But you know I've got a chimp in the shed if you wanna see that. I can show him to you and your daughter if you'd like."

"A chimp, you say?"

And he says, "Yup." And then he says, "He's pretty old, though." He said that like he was warning us, like he didn't want us to be disappointed.

So I asked your mommy, "You wanna see a chimpanzee?" and she did, of course, so we went to see the guy's chimp.

Turned out that the shed was a fair walk from where we were, back through a bunch of machinery sheds and old equipment and grain bins, and then a ways across through this old pumpkin graveyard, rotted pumpkins all over the place. Well, I was holding your mommy's hand and helping her wade through the weeds, and I was having second thoughts. To tell the truth, I got a little nervous about that old man all of a sudden, because I didn't really know him. If I were on my own, then going into some stranger's shed might be okay, but I had your mommy there to think about, and I don't know, but my imagination got away from me. I started to think that he might not have a chimp in that shed at all. All of a sudden, I had the clear image that maybe he'd have some hitchhiker he'd picked up, and he'd have that hitchhiker all tied up. So I started getting kinda antsy. And then when we came up on that shed, I saw a big pile of sawed-off antlers there. They looked like a pile of bones, and that didn't give me any comfort at all.

Kris fooled with the padlock while I stood there and stared at those antlers, and then we went into the shed, and we saw there was a chimp in there, all right. He was hunkered over in a big cage, and he had a red-hot potbellied stove blazing next to him. He wasn't moving, though. He was staring at the wall like he was pouting about something. There were bushels and bushels of baskets of green tomatoes and old potatoes and carrots beside the cage, and there were the chewed-up remains of potatoes and green tomatoes all over the floor! Your mommy was disgusted. You should've seen her. I'd give ten whole dollars right now for the look on her face.

Kris starts saying, "Now don't let your little girl get too close! Don't get close now. Because this here animal spits!" And almost like the chimp understood, he jumped up and spit out pieces of chewed-up carrot and then showed us his teeth. I couldn't tell if he was happy or just being a smart-ass. "Now don't get too close," Kris says.

The chimp bit into a tomato, chewed it up real careful, and started spitting that toward us, too. Spraying it, really. And Kris got mad at him and he says, "Now see here!" and he says, "You there. You cut that out!" and he raised his hand, and the chimp seemed to flinch and duck, and so I wondered whether or not Kris beat that chimp, but I didn't say anything about it.

Kris says, "Oh, he only acts like that when strangers are around. He's just an old faker really. He won't hurt anyone" And to prove this, Kris walked right up to the cage and put his hand inside.

Let me tell you, that made me so nervous that I picked up your mommy and held her. I almost couldn't stand it. I just wanted to scoop her up and get the hell out of there. But then you know, just as soon as Kris put his arm in the cage, that chimp kinda petted it. And then the chimp reached though the bars real careful and patted Kris on the shoulder, and I thought, Well, that looks sweet. Like there was some affection between them.

But then I noticed how much Kris was shaking. And I noticed how slowly each of them was moving, like they didn't want to spook each other with any fast movements. Then I could see that the only reason why they were so careful with each other was because they didn't hardly trust each other at all. I could see that plain. Finally Kris pulled his arm away from the chimp and stood back, and he says to me, "Care to guess how old he is?"

I couldn't really tell. The chimp was kinda gray around the muzzle, but I didn't have the basis for any comparison. "He's fifteen years old," Kris says, sounding like he was bragging about it. "And I've had him since he was two. And he used to have a mate, too, but she died young. She got a cough one night when the stove went out."

I looked at that chimp sitting there looking bored and depressed, and I asked Kris if he ever let the chimp out, and Kris says, "No. Not much at least. Not for a long time."

Well, that kinda got to me, too. It was the same thing as with the Nighthawk, that beautiful car sitting out in the open and rotting in the sun, and here that chimp was being kept in a cage. This Kris guy just wanted to know where they were, just wanted to hang onto them and own them. He didn't really care about them. And the Nighthawk was one thing, but this was a living creature, so I said to him, "You know, it's not too late now. Maybe that chimp would appreciate being let out once in a while."

To tell the truth, I didn't think what I said would matter to this Kris so much, but right off he got this kinda guilty look. Or maybe it was kind of a perplexed look. I mean he looked like he was studying the point, like he never thought of it before, and pretty soon he says, "Well, I—"

But then he was quiet and studying the point again.

"Well, . . . I just don't know," he says.

I was standing there, waiting for him to just get it out, when I noticed that the chimp's hair was thin on his rump, like a pair of pants gone out in the seat. Like the chimp spent a lot of time just sitting there.

"Well, you know," he says. "I . . . I just might do that. But . . . I don't know. What's there to do around here anyway? You know my brother was always saying he was bored, too. Nothing to do. So he goes off to that war, and he never comes back, so then I start in to thinking, That's what looking for excitement will get you. Ain't worth the bother. We didn't even get his body back."

That's what he said. I saw it was pretty much useless to try to talk to him about it. Those old farmers usually want to do things their own way and not be meddled with. "But I want you to know that we don't mistreat this animal," Kris says. "No sirree. I want you to know that we hose him down real often, and you can see that he gets plenty of food. You just look at him. He's got good fur. There ain't a bit of the mange on that chimp, and that's a fact. Take a look and see for yourself."

I admitted that I knew enough about animals that I could see its fur was good. I didn't doubt that he took good care of it, and I told him so. I just thought he should let the chimp out once in a while. But Kris seemed to be stuck on the fact of whether or not the animal was healthy. Kris says, "I want you to take a good look at that animal, and if that animal has any mange, well then, I want you to lock me up, too! Come on. Step up here and look at him."

So then I admitted that I didn't really care to. I said that I could see the animal well enough from where I was, and I didn't really want to get any closer.

"Oh, come on up here. Good Lord! Take a look at this chimp. Your daughter, too. He's calmed down by now."

"I think we'll have to pass up on that," I said.

"Oh, come on now," he says. "He's not gonna hurt anyone."

"No," I said. "No, we really can't do that. And we really have to be going now."

Well, when I said that, Kris just stared at me with a hurt look in his eye. From the way he looked you'd think I'd insulted him.

"I suppose you think we don't treat that animal right," he finally says. "Well I want you to know that it just ain't true. You're not being fair to me or this chimp!"

And like he was gonna prove his point, all of a sudden this Kris grabbed a box of flea powder. He stepped toward the cage like he was getting ready to give that chimp a fresh dusting, and right away that chimp got a wide-eyed look and he got up on his back legs like he was getting ready to protect himself. The chimp showed his teeth and bounced back and forth on his heels with his arms up in the air, bouncing up and down and making these angry chimp sounds, a lot of hooting with some screaming. And when Kris got close enough, one of the chimp's arms shot out of that cage, and that chimp had a reach! I guessed that he wanted to grab the box of flea powder and get it away from Kris, but it didn't work. Kris doused that animal with white powder anyway, and the chimp cried out, and then, real slow, he sat back on his haunches and lowered his head, and he hunched down low and still, like he was humiliated.

What could we do then? I just said to Kris that we'd probably bothered him enough, and he didn't act like he was inclined to disagree. He says, "Oh? Oh, okay. Well, okay. But could you wait for a second? Just give me a second, and I'll be right with you."

You know, I've always had a hard time ending a conversation. You could probably say that it's a fault of mine. So I carried your mommy outside and we waited, just to shake this guy's hand and tell him thank you, really, because that's how I was raised. So I stood there and waited, letting my eyes rest on that pile of sawed-off antlers. I put your mommy down.

Those antlers were about waist deep and so dense they looked like they growed there. Your mommy walked over to them, and she picked one of the antlers up. She just picked it up and looked at it. I said, "Put it down, sweetheart," because I knew by now that this old man was particular and wouldn't want anything on his farm disturbed. And your mommy was reluctant, but she minded me, like she always did. But the way she stared at those antlers I knew that she really wanted to pick one out, so I thought I might as well ask this Kris for one, as a keepsake you know, but I never got the chance to, because pretty soon he came back out of the shed holding on to that chimp's hand and leading him. The chimp kinda waddled beside him. Kris says, "See here? This chimp won't hurt no one."

Well, I practically shouted at Kris then. I said, "I really didn't mean that you should let him out while we were here!" And I went to grab hold of your mommy again, but before I could do it, that chimp broke free and scooted for the pile of antlers. Soon as he got there, he put two of them on his head, and your mommy just giggled. She really thought that was funny.

"We used to have lots of animals," Kris says. "It was my brother who started me buying them and all. We had a llama and a Brahma bull and some wild animals, too, deer and elk. But I killed them all. About ten years ago. We had this little silver fox that folks really thought was real cute. Everyone was always coming out to have pictures of their kids taken with that fox. And everything was fine until the fox bit this little girl. And then, dammit, all hell broke loose."

I looked over at your mommy when Kris said that, and I saw that the chimp was lightly touching her hair with his fingertips. I tell you, I didn't like that at all. At first she stood there and let him do it, but then she stepped back, and the chimp jerked back his paw, too, like he'd touched something hot.

I said, "You know, I really wish you'd keep an eye on that chimp of yours."

But Kris kept on talking. Thank God that the chimp got bored quick. He waddled over behind Kris and stood there with his hands on Kris's kneecaps, and he looked at me from between Kris's legs, peeling back his lips and grinning, but Kris didn't seem to notice him.

Kris says, "First off I find out that her daddy's a sheriff, and he starts in raising hell, and so we had to kill the fox and have its head sent in to check for rabies. Well, I just couldn't stand it. Been here all my life, never had any trouble in the world, but then people start to meddle with you, and it ain't ever the same. So I just killed the whole lot of them, just in one day, from sunrise to sunset, and they were all dead then except for that chimp and the birds. I was trying to kill the birds, too, but I just couldn't seem to catch them. I wouldn't ever dream of killing that chimp, though. I guess you could say that chimp owes me his life. Seemed like a dream, I was so angry. I was running around with a shot-gun, all in a fever to get it done, and it didn't take hardly nothing to do it, either. Most of those animals I just burned up in a big fire at the end of the day. Kept those antlers, though. I don't know why."

And that was his story.

"How about that," I said. "Well, we'd best be going now."

About then, the chimp crawled all the way through Kris's legs and held out his arms to Kris, but Kris says, "No, no, you're too big, understand? I can't carry you." But he did take that chimp's hand, and the two of them walked us to our car.

I could see that your mommy really liked that chimp. She didn't want to get very close to him, though, and that was fine with me. I started liking that chimp myself, especially after he ran off those geese when they got too close. I also liked it when he got a twig and started digging up an ant pile. He sure knew how to amuse himself.

I gave Kris one more chance. "So you gonna sell me that car?" But he knew I was just kidding. He smiled and shook my hand, and we drove away, and that's the last I ever saw of him, but you know something? On the way home, your mama was talking to her pumpkins like they were her babies, and that night after we got home, we carved those pumpkins out and made a bunch of jack-o-lanterns, and we dumped the seeds and goop out behind our house, in this empty lot, and about a million pumpkins grew up the next year, all of them twisted and lop-sided like there was something wrong with them. Nothing was, though. They were all interesting to look at. And they made a good pie.

Bookworm

I FIRST STARTED to draw apart from my neighbors as a child. I would hide inside our small library, a confused little building built by the WPA, where keystones topped the wood-framed windows. I hid there throughout most of my childhood. My hometown grew as ghostly to me as an old couple who did not feel the need to talk anymore. You see, there is nothing here to look at other than the convex sky and the geometrically flat ground. Tourists grow dizzy in the presence of our sky and quickly grab their car doors to keep from floating off. I see them down by the interstate, taking careful steps beside their cars, watching their feet as if to keep their balance.

At first, angered by the ambiguities and the hypocrisy of my hometown, I planned to leave it, as many small-town children do. But as it turned out, I never did, for upon reaching the age of majority, I found a job as the clerk in a mail-order catalog store. People would come in, search through the catalog. I would fill out their orders to give the enterprise a human touch, and that was that. It was a comfortable arrangement: I could read all day long, occasionally calling customers to inform them that some object had materialized, a washer, a bicycle, the word of the catalog becoming flesh as it were. And that was that. So, you see, I've lived most of my life under a gooseneck lamp, a mixed metaphor for sunflower, a heliotrope in its own right, but I was one who was only attracted to the word "sun" when justified in columns of Roman type.

As a teenager, I felt I had discovered a pattern to my little library that in its particulars made sense but that defeated me in the overall. For example, I could not find a single book about the original inhabitants of our land. On the other hand, there was a preponderance of old theosophy texts, with its odd blearing of occultism, eastern faiths, and western armchair anthropology. Over time, the library grew smaller, so small that I hardly used it for anything more than accessing interlibrary loan.

I can honestly say that I have read every book in the place. I've continued to read every book as it has arrived. I never talked to anyone about any of these books, not even the old woman who was the librarian of my childhood years.

I remember how she used to look at me every time I came in, as if she knew something I had yet to discover. The door would open; the hot summer air and the sound of cicadas would pour into the library with me. I was a neat little child, dressed for Sunday School every day of the week. She would look up from her own book and smile, looking very sad, as if her sadness were the one thing that the books could never describe, and so—therefore—she could never stop searching for it in those books. We never spoke. And then she died.

And then I became the librarian. In all these years, not a chair, not a table has been moved. I never changed a thing about the place, not even the elementary filing system. In the back of each book, there was a card that you signed. The library retained this card to ensure the book's return. I rather enjoyed this method of doing business. When you picked up a book, you could read a list of everyone in town who had read the book before, plus the date when they read it. Although I never had the urge to trace these people, it was nice to know that, if I ever wanted to, I could. It created a dull sense of community; however, it was not unusual to see a twenty-year gap between my reading and someone else's, or even to see my name all alone among the empty decades, the sole inhabitant of a community of one.

This system, of course, had its drawbacks. I must admit that when I first became librarian, I worried whether this system would play right into the hands of those people who believed in the corrupting influence of certain books. Sure enough, the fundamentalist ministers, those annoying individuals who take a word at its word, would often search the library cards of the very few scandalous books in our collection. They would search the library cards for lost souls. I often wondered why they did not petition me to remove these books. I would have honored their request, if they had only asked. What did I care? But, surprisingly, they didn't. I suppose this was because they took more joy in discovering who would be tempted to read books such as these than in preventing the books from being read in the first place, and I saw no reason to discourage their efforts. A public library is free and open to anyone.

Recently, however, a remarkable thing has happened that very much confirmed for me the impression that some books do in fact have a corrupting influence. It began when I discovered a lost book, a book that had long been buried behind a row of books, like foreign matter in a closed scar. It was called The Conqueror Worm, the title from the poem by Poe, of course. What's more, the library card revealed that it had only been checked out once, by a Mildred Weber, over fifty years ago.

The sound of the spine crackling open set off sympathetic harmonies in my own spine, but I delayed my pleasure. I took the book home with me and read it that evening, delving into the strange obsessions of an author long dead. On page 37, there was a dried leaf, a maple. On page 98, I found the burrow of a long-dead creature. Aside from these distractions, calling me to the world of shapes and sounds and creatures, I must admit that I enjoyed The Conqueror Worm tremendously. The language was pleasingly abstract, utterly lacking loud noises and bright lights, a calm and quiet document. The woman listed on the title page as the author—a certain Emily Kraft—had the good sense to leave all biographical notes off the liner. The book existed, as it were, in a room of its own, lacking all reference to anything that mattered, enjoying its solitude.

It was the story of a Norwegian gravedigger, who lovingly described the contortions of death and the solemnity of her work. I do not know for sure, but I think it was this woman's memoir—something about the episodic structure, a life where we get the high points only as she dances from one blithe anecdote about grave digging to another. You could tell that she clearly thought her stories where amusing and cute, as if she didn't realize how ghastly they were: caskets bursting open, dogs creeping into the graveyard after a flu epidemic, a series of comedies about confused identities such as one man being buried beside another man's wife—and all this in the sentimental tone of inspirational literature, told in homilies and anecdotes.

I admit that this does not sound like a good book at all, but I enjoyed it thoroughly. It was a book that remained well fixed between its sturdy covers. It never taxed me by forcing an examination of my life or those around me. A book that knew it was a book, and nothing more. A document profoundly and movingly solipsistic. As weeks went by, I found that I would pick up The Conqueror Worm time and again, returning to its padded cells, its utter irrelevance, with a kind of relief. In fact, I enjoyed the book so much that something happened to me that's never happened to me before. I wanted to contact the book's previous reader, this Mildred Weber.

The truth is, I'd never heard of her before, an unusual thing, although not impossible, in a town of three thousand. I actually began to imagine conversations with her about this book. Then it happened one day that one of those ministers, a so-called man of the Word, wandered into the library to examine our latest books on the occult. I saw him smile as he pulled out his notebook and began to write down names of the curious, the lost, the sick in spirit, and the merely spooky. But as he began to handle an older book, he suddenly looked perplexed and said to me aloud: "Do you know a Mrs. Mildred Weber?"

I looked at the library card in his hand, and there was her name again, in one of those theosophy texts I mentioned before, a book called Out of Body. I had to smile, remembering how I enjoyed these unlikely little tales as a child, with their glowing tunnels and ectoplastic cords of light. As I reread the book that very evening, I felt clothed in the seamless robes of gullibility again.

Despite extensive research, all I was able to learn about Mildred Weber was that she had outlived three husbands. She lived north of town in the part of the country known as "Table," which some maps still show as a town occupying the interstice of two seldom-used country roads—but of course the town itself vanished years ago. The road to her house was a debased path of asphalt deteriorating into gravel, gravel dissolving into dirt. The house itself looked abandoned, but I knocked on the door anyway, and I waited forever. As I was about to walk away, an old woman opened the door just a little. She stared at me, bewildered, through spectacles so thick that her eyes were a blur. But then she recognized me. "Oh," she said. "You're that young bookworm I've heard so much about!"

I cannot tell you how much I hate that phrase, which haunted me through my childhood. But I restrained myself. She gave a laugh that in other contexts might be described as musical and charming; but in this context, with the wind howling, and the loose boards of her house shuddering in a grand mal seizure, her laugh can only be said to be chilling, like a nail being pulled out of dense wood. "Come in! Come in!" she said. "I've been waiting for you."

I stepped into the wind-stripped cabin that she called her home. Immediately, walls upon walls of books confronted me. The books were packed into every available space, perched upon windowsills and cabinets, climbing over the doorjambs, growing from the middle of the floor in dangerous stacks that leaned against the air. Then there was the smell. I know the smell of old books, and this was all that and more. My powers of description seem to have failed me right now, but mustering a few generalizations, let me call it musty, or stuffy, or dank. But add to that the smell of stale smoke, and scorched coffee, and the hint of something not so recently dead.

She served me coffee in a foul and crusty cup, veined by dangerous little cracks. It was a fearful brew, the very cup of suffering. I glanced around at the titles and did not notice a single volume of fiction.

Histories, mythology, theology, poetry, science, even theosophy, as well
as other arcane studies—but no fiction. I asked her about this, somewhat
idly, not knowing what else to say to a woman who was obviously out
of her mind. Recluses like myself are often burdened with exceedingly
good manners, and I thought it would be rude to leave so soon.

"Fiction?" she said. "Fiction? Oh, no. No fiction for me. I read just
one novel many years back, and then I became very sick, from just that
one. 'No more!' I said. That novel killed my husbands, you see, and it
almost killed me, but I was too clever, too . . . hardy! I survived! And
the irony," she added, "is that my dear husbands didn't even read the
book. By that time the book had infected me and I was—how do you
say? The carrier? The vector? Perhaps I am too slow a reader. A quick
reader might have avoided the worm."

"The worm?" I said.

"Well, you would not be here unless you discovered *The Conqueror
Worm* now, would you?"

Her observation astonished me.

"Oh dear. You have, haven't you. I had really hoped to contact you
before you actually read the book, but alas, I have been negligent, as
always. I'm so very sorry! I am such a lazy girl, as my mother and father
always said. They did not feel that reading books constituted work,
much less an avocation. But then I don't have to tell you how people
look at us bookworms, do I?"

"I am not a bookworm," I said. I couldn't help but notice a childish
tone in my voice.

"Perhaps not. Perhaps . . . not! But you certainly are a host to one!
He resides within you, wriggling and conspiring!"

I stared at her. I had no idea what she was saying except that she,
somehow, was attempting to get my goat. "I don't have to stand for
these insults," I said, "so I think I really should be going."

"Oh, I am not speaking figuratively. The worm inside you is real, I
assure you. An *ascaris lumbricoides*. I am speaking of the American round-
worm, which often lives in the dust of old books. You are most certainly
infested. Already the eggs are in your duodenum, hatching. Poking out
their tiny heads, looking around, looking around! They are no doubt
happy to be awake after their long sleep! Soon, however, they will grow
restless! They will penetrate the wall of your intestine, work their way
into your heart via the liver, and then be whisked away into the lungs.
It seems to me that this part would be great fun, like riding on a water
slide! There they will rest and molt before climbing the windpipe to
your mouth, where you will swallow them. Then they go back to your
small intestine to mate and begin the process all over! Isn't it marvelous,

the sweep of it! The circle of nature! And I understand that under a microscope, they are very pretty creatures! You see, I was infected first, and then I infected one husband, then the other. I infected them repeatedly. Their constitutions could not take it. Would you like some toast? You must feed the worm, you know. Books are not enough for this one, since he's such a long and very hungry worm. Do you know the poem by Poe?"

She stepped back from me and assumed the oratorical pose of a lost century and declaimed:

"'But see, amid the mimic rout / A crawling shape intrude!' The 'mimic rout' may seem obscure, but is it not a good image for a library, where fools such as we are routed and ravened by a book's mimicry? 'A blood-red thing that writhes from out / The scenic solitude!' Oh how we have longed for this, this solitude. But the worm looks for community, a host. The worm is a guest. 'It writhes!—it writhes!—with mortal pangs / The mimes become its food. . . .' And who are 'the mimes,' my boy? Who are 'the mimes'?"

Suddenly, Mrs. Mildred Weber ceased her recitation and looked confused. Perhaps she did not remember what came next in the poem. She hurried to a pile of books packed into her window frame, and I watched as she began to pry loose a book residing low in the stack. For an old woman, she was quite determined about this, clenching her face, turning red. I watched as the tall pile of books began to lean and totter dangerously as she freed a book and opened it, and before I could warn her, the books collapsed altogether, a sudden avalanche. Sunlight poured into the room through the open window. I stood there, stunned by the sight: a V of geese, a scrawl of clouds. Mrs. Mildred Weber also seemed to be surprised, disturbed, even threatened by the world outside her cabin. "Oh my," she said. "Why, is it spring already?" I felt the first wave of nausea. I have felt it every night since. I feel it even now as I recall how she stood, clutching the slender volume in her hand, her finger buried between the pages to keep her place.

The Stanley Andrews Story

IF GEORGE AND DARROW hated anybody at all—and most times it seemed they hated everybody—it was Stanley Andrews. He lived nearby, right outside of Brady, between the train tracks and the river, but mostly now he toured all over the country with his band, who called themselves the Sundowners and were a country-and-western group. He was on the road a lot, but he might be back for a month at a time, and then he might occasionally play the Cowpoke Inn. "Just to return a favor to those people who helped to make me what I am," he'd say. "And to let you know I ain't ever forgot you."

He was a humble guy for all he'd been able to do, and that's just the kind of thing about him that'd drive George and Darrow nuts. As the years passed, I thought of those two a lot, everyone did, their names tied to Stanley Andrews forever and forever. They hated him something fierce, but that didn't keep those boys from showing up wherever he was playing—only they claimed they were casing the place. "Yeah, like one of these days we're gonna hang that goat-roper," Darrow would say.

"Nothing personal," George'd say. "But what he does to a good country song's gotta be paid for."

"It's nothing personal at all."

But we weren't so sure. They always acted like their hatred of Stanley Andrews was serving some kind of public service, but we all liked Stanley. No one could really seem to figure it out. If Stanley Andrews said something like, "Here's an old tune by the late, great Hank Williams," they'd heckle him. One of them would yell out, "Late? Hell, I thought he was dead!" Whether Stanley Andrews heard them or not, you couldn't tell. I guess he didn't let on. But like I say, most people liked him because he looked like he'd been places. He had a blue coat with white shoulders and pockets, blue boots with white toe and heel, and a blue cowboy hat, a nice one, with a white hatband. He'd say things like, "And here's a song that the folks in Kansas City really go for. It's called 'Honky Tonkin'."

It's not often that you can feel as if you're watching history being made, but that's how I felt whenever I saw Stanley Andrews play. He was a real professional. You could tell it by the way he joked with his band, or the way he could go somber all of a sudden for one of those "talkin' songs" about highway ghosts and such. Then he'd do a medley of TV western theme songs, ending with "Rawhide," which really got the blood moving, but the highlight of the evening was the Hank Williams memorial medley. He'd stand with his hat in his hand and do a dedication to Hank while his band played the Indian tom-tom beat that begins "Kaw-liga." Then after he told about how Hank lived and died and how many songs he wrote and how all the world loved him, he would wave the downbeat and they would start in with "Your Cheatin' Heart" and then go through all the saddest songs Hank ever wrote.

And Stanley Andrews wouldn't even open his eyes. He had the shake and the squeak in the voice just right, and he could make it break like it should, right when the song got emotional. He was something else. And he knew every train song that'd ever been written. Fact is that, besides singing Hank Williams, train songs were his specialty, which kind of tied him to the history of our town, where trains were always passing through. If it weren't for trains, we wouldn't even be here. And no one had any doubt that the sound of the train whistle would set him off thinking of all the places it was going that we would never ever get. No one, that is, excepting George and Darrow. You'd see those two boys standing in the crowd whenever the Sundowners were in town, looking miserable—looking like they wanted to slap themselves around if they couldn't find anyone else to slap.

Since they made no secret of their plans to do Stanley Andrews in, I asked them about it one night when I was standing around with a bunch of local boys, and Darrow said this: "Well, he don't know trains and he don't know trucks, and he don't know a heifer from a steer, and he don't know sorghum from milo, and he don't even know much about music from the sound of him. So it ain't nothing personal, but someday that goat-roper's gonna die, and we're gonna be scarce, and that's my personal word of honor."

Someone suggested that maybe George and Darrow just felt disadvantaged when Stanley Andrews was around, because of the attention the women paid him, and George said, "You don't take that serious, do you? That's just all show, all that oohin' and aahin's just part of the act.

After the show's over, those women go home and feel embarrassed about it, like those women squealing over Elvis."

"It's those mop-heads now," I said.

"Still don't matter. That's what you call showbiz," Darrow said, giving me an evil look, "and it don't mean nothing."

"Well, I don't know," I said. "I saw him with three women one night, and I said to him that he should bring me along, share the wealth, you know. But he said he couldn't do that, because then those women would figure out all the lies he's been telling them. Well, I told him I could lie and cheat as well as the next guy, but he said I hadn't had the right training, since my folks were such good people."

It sparked everyone that someone like Stanley Andrews would hand out compliments like this. Someone said, "You'd think all that fame would've gone to his head."

"No, sir. Says he just got lucky."

"Lucky ain't the word for it. Hell, people gonna talk about him and Hank in the same breath. He's gonna be a legend in his own time, I swear! And we're all gonna be able to say we knew him way back when! I wouldn't be surprised if he ran for public office someday."

For all their plans to do Stanley in, Darrow and George shut up and sat still, trying not to act like they listened to this talk. But they did. They listened to every word. And the next time Stanley Andrews and the Sundowners played at the Poke, those two boys were there like everybody else.

"Howdy, folks! Glad to see so many friends in the audience. You know me, I'm Stanley Andrews, and we are the Sundowners!"

The dance floor was crowded with folks getting ready to do their swing two-step and jitterbug, old and young alike. Stanley started in with "Settin' the Woods on Fire," only he did it with a growl in his voice, kind of soulful sounding, to show he didn't have to do it like Hank did. Some people said that he was doing Hank one better. It didn't matter that they'd heard these songs before, because Stanley Andrews could make them sound like he just thought them up. Almost everyone'd seen *Your Cheatin' Heart: The Hank Williams Story* over at the Sun Theater, and they were talking about that scene where Hank's forced to sing at a gospel picnic, just to get something to eat, and all he knows is honky-tonk, and so he's against the wall and has to make up "I Saw the Light" right on the spot. Every song that Stanley Andrews sang sounded like that, like it'd come fresh into his head.

I was there that night, so I saw some of this myself and the rest I got by word of mouth. I mean around here you can't have an itch without someone else trying to scratch it, so I know pretty much exactly what happened. Especially after I coaxed Harry Markin into telling the rest of the story—and he was pretty much scared to repeat it for fear it'd get back to those boys' next of kin, who were pretty much as mean as they were. Anyway, as you'd expect, George and Darrow came sashaying into the Poke like they were surprised there was something going on. It was in the middle of irrigation season, and they both had hip-waders on and mud on their shirts.

Darrow said, "Well, if it ain't Stanley and the Andrews Sisters."

"Stanley and the Spam-Canners," George said.

"Stanley Antler and the Hung-downers. Oh, look at them boots. Don't think he's ever got manure on them, you think?"

"He's got manure in them clear up till the top of his head."

"Boy, it'd be a shame if they buried that guy. Just throw him in a manure spreader and cover a couple acres."

They forced their way to the front so that they were standing in the middle of the dance floor. "Hey, there's Harry," George said. "Go over and grab him." Darrow walked over to the other side of the dance floor and grabbed Harry Markin by the back of the neck.

"Hey, Darrow! Ouch! How're ya doing?" Harry was scrunching up his shoulders, trying to relieve the pressure of Darrow's grip.

"How'd you like your neck broke?" Darrow asked him.

"Not much, I don't think."

"George says you've been looking for me, saying you got a score to settle."

"That ain't so, Darrow."

"You're not calling George a liar, are ya?"

"Uh-uh. No, sir!"

"Well, I think you oughta come over and explain things to me and him. I mean, we're kinda hurt about it. Kinda mad, 'cause we always thought of you and us as friends."

"Well, we are! Sure we are, mostly."

"I'd like to think so, Harry. Just step over here and we'll settle this." Darrow took Harry by the arm and led him to the other side of the dance floor, where George was standing, arms crossed, cradling his beer. When he saw Harry, a pained look came across his face. "Dammit, Harry, I told you I didn't want any more trouble."

"Harry's calling you a liar, George."

"No, I didn't. I said no such thing."

"See what I'm talking about? Now he's calling me a liar."

George said, "Why're you calling my brother a liar, Harry?"

"I'm not saying anything else. Nothing. If you guys want to beat me up, go 'head, 'cause I see it coming and I can't do anything 'bout it."

"Beat you up?" George looked hurt again. "Why would we beat you up?" He gestured with his bottle toward the stage. "That fool in the spotlight's the real problem. Since when did they put a spotlight in the Poke?"

Harry was wedged in between them with no place to run, so he told them that the spotlight came from Stanley Andrews himself, who was finishing up singing about cool, clear water. People were slow dancing, and then there was a burst of applause and foot stomping as the Sundowners started in with "Ring of Fire."

"Damn!" Darrow gave a kick at the floor. "And I liked that song, too."

"So, Harry. Are you telling me that Stanley Andrews gave us all that spotlight for him to stand in? And we're all supposed to be thankful?"

"Stanley says this is his favorite place to play in the whole world," Harry said, "and he wanted to show the people at the Poke he meant it. Makes it look like a big-city club."

"What is he, ashamed of us? Has to pretend he's somewhere else?"

"Oh, no! No one thinks that about Stanley Andrews. He's never got too big for his friends. Everyone says that."

Stanley Andrews finished the song and there was more applause and foot stomping, and when that died down he never started in with the next song. He just talked for a while.

"Thank you ever so much. It does me proud to have you come out here and see me off, 'cause me and the Sundowners are going on the road again, and when I'm out there in Wichita and Lawrence and K.C. and Jefferson City and Omaha and Des Moines, I'm gonna think back on tonight and that's what's gonna keep me going." He paused for a while. "Could someone turn down this spotlight?" At the mention of the spotlight everyone started applauding, and Stanley said, "That spot's my gift, 'cause I want you to remember me, but it makes it kinda hard to see you while I'm up here." Someone turned it down, and he said, "There, now I can see you all. We have time for one last song, so what's it gonna be?"

"'Lovesick Blues,'" someone called.

"'Window Shoppin''!"

"'Your Cheatin' Heart'!"

"Drop Dead!"

"What's that? Sorry, couldn't hear that."

People around Darrow and George shushed them so they didn't repeat it.

"Did someone say 'Cheatin' Heart'?" Stanley Andrews turned around and smiled at his band. "Didn't we already play that one, Sundowners?"

"Play it again," someone yelled, and everyone cheered.

"Okay. All right. Thank you, everyone. Thank you much. So here's another one by the legendary Hank Williams, and it's called 'Your Cheatin' Heart'! Are you ready, Sundowners?"

Headly Fergusson and "Sleepy" Helmquist grinned at each other and nodded like they always do while Stanley counted off the beat, and Collin Watson, who'd been with Stanley from the very beginning, started up with the Hawaiian guitar introduction. Stanley said, "Now I want everyone to sing along, 'cause I'm feeling mighty lonesome up here tonight."

"Lonesome?" Darrow said. "Hell, he's practically crowding everyone else off the stage! If he's lonesome, it's because of that umbrella of a hat he has!"

"Jesus, let's get out of here," George said. "I'm so sick I feel like shooting someone. You coming with us, Harry?"

Harry didn't have much to say about it. They walked him outside where the streets were quiet and empty, not a car or pickup on the road. Someone passing through might have thought the town was deserted, except for the muffled sound of music and the people singing along.

"Hell," George said. "By the time we drive anywhere else, everything's gonna be closed."

They stood there in the street, not moving anywhere.

"So what we gonna do?" Harry asked.

Darrow and George looked at each other.

"We're gonna go back and wait by Stanley Shitkicker's bus," George said. "We've gotta talk business with him."

At this point, Harry said he distinctly saw Darrow pull a gun out and check the chamber. "Yeah, Harry," Darrow said. "We got a song we wrote. Think it'll be a hit and we want to give him first turndown."

"It's called 'Spotlight Blues,'" George said.

"It's about how lonesome it is to be a country-and-western star."

After the music ended, they heard the sound of pickups and cars starting up. There was a lot of laughing, people revving their motors. Harry wanted to run, but he was too scared. After a while the Sundowners were coming out with trunks and amps and guitars. One of them—I think it was Sleepy—asked if Darrow and George and Harry were waiting for anyone.

"Sure," George said. "We're waiting for Stanley."

"Well, he'll be out in a little while. He's pretty tired, though. Is this important?"

"Sure. It's a life-and-death matter," Darrow said.

Sleepy looked at them. "You're kidding, right?"

"Oh hell, yes," George said. "We're just a couple of local jokers."

"What we really want is Stanley's autograph. We're collectors. We got Johnny Cash's and Jim Reeves's and all of them. We figure Stanley Andrews is gonna be like them someday."

Right then Stanley Andrews came out with a woman next to him. They looked like they were fighting about something. At least Stanley Andrews was pleading with her, promising all kinds of reformations for whatever she was accusing him of doing. Harry told me it was a long list: drinking, whoring, throwing his money around, never being around—almost embarrassing for George and Darrow to listen to, and she was chewing him out good. Then he stopped there in the middle of the alley and lit a strange-smelling cigarette. It was years and years until we figured out what that was.

"Mr. Andrews," George called.

"What? Who's that?"

"Don't you recognize us, Mr. Andrews?"

Stanley Andrews walked up to them and looked them over. "Uh, the faces are familiar but I can't put a name to . . ." Then he stopped. "Oh yeah. You're Darrow and, ah, George Drumlin. Yeah, I believe your folks and mine were friends."

"I'm Harry Markin," Harry said.

"Glad to meet you, Harry. So. What can I do for you boys?"

Of a sudden George and Darrow had nothing to say. I guess they hadn't expected Stanley to remember them, which kind of changed everything. Harry looked at both of them, and they looked at each other. Stanley said, "Look, my hands are kinda full right now." But those two boys were still pretty quiet. Harry Markin said it was the most unnatural thing he ever saw.

Finally Darrow said, "All we wanted was to thank you for the spotlight, Mr. Andrews."

"Mighty smart spotlight," George said.

Stanley Andrews looked at them with a blank look. Then he started laughing. He exchanged looks with the woman, who was still angry, not at all impressed with this show of gratitude. "How 'bout that, baby? They wanted to thank me for the spotlight."

George and Darrow stood there like they had metal rods up their sleeves and down their pant legs and one down the back of their necks, not knowing what to say.

"So tell me," Stanley said, "which of you is George and which is Darrow? Never could keep you two straight."

George said, "He's Darrow, I'm George."

"I'm Harry," Harry said.

"Well, see you around," Stanley Andrews said. He climbed halfway into the bus and then stopped and gave them a final wave. Harry said that wave looked like the wave someone gives when they know there's going to be a photograph of it in every newspaper tomorrow morning, kind of a sweeping wave, kind of a this-is-for-eternity wave, and when he climbed into that bus he climbed out of our lives and into history.

❀　　❀　　❀

So now it comes to my part. The part of the story I play. I was sitting there in the Poke the next night looking over the newspaper, wondering why there wasn't a word in it about what happened to Stanley Andrews. Plenty about that Lee Harvey Oswald though. Oswald was getting to be about as famous as Kennedy was. Anyway, I was there when Darrow and George managed to drag themselves into the bar. And I knew what they were walking into, almost like I could see the future, and so I sat there and watched.

"What goes?" George asked the bartender. There were a lot of people there, standing around and looking at the stage, and there was that spotlight, shining on nothing. "Stanley and the Rum-rounders gonna play again?"

"Jesus help me," Darrow said.

The bartender never looked at them. He said, "What, you boys just get up or something?"

"Hell no, we've been working our butts off!"

"Well, then you haven't heard. And if I were you I'd try to keep it quiet. It's nothing to joke about."

Then the bartender motioned for them to come over. He pointed at the spotlight.

"He's dead," he said. "Happened last night real late. People say he was walking down the train tracks and got hit."

"He's dead?"

"People talking like it had to've been suicide. I suppose we expected too much of him. Expecting him to take on all our sorrow, all our sad stories. Showing his sad, sad heart to everyone night after night, just so we could go home feeling happy. That must have been what happened, and it got to be too much for him to handle. Either that, or he was walking down the train tracks and wasn't paying attention. . . . Anyways, that's why we got that spotlight on. He said it was so we'll remember him, and we sure will. That spotlight's all that's left of him."

"Sure is if a train hit him."

We all looked at that empty spotlight on the empty stage. There were people gathered around, talking quietly. Someone put a Hank Williams song on the jukebox—"Your Cheatin' Heart."

"You know," the bartender said, wiping away a tear, "it's like that final scene in *Your Cheatin' Heart: The Hank Williams Story*. You see that? After Hank died and they announced it at the concert, people started singing all the songs he wrote. It wasn't planned or nothing. They just sang them and looked at the empty spotlight on the stage, where Hank was supposed to be, but won't be no more."

I could hear someone crying and someone comforting someone else. Hank's thin voice and all that emotion went all through the bar. I was gulping at my beer, barely able to get it past the lump in my throat, but mainly trying to look like I was minding my own business as I listened in. The bartender finally got a hold of himself and said, "Yup, it's exactly like in *The Hank Williams Story*. Way I figure it is that history was made last night. Right here. The final performance of Stanley Andrews and the Sundowners. Course they're taking it hard. They won't be able to find anyone to replace him. He was the whole show."

George leaned over to Darrow and I heard him whisper, "Brother, I feel lucky tonight."

Darrow asked the bartender, "So where'd this happen?"

"By the river crossing, next to his place."

"Give us a case," Darrow said. "I think I'm too upset to drink in public."

It was then that George caught me staring at them. I froze up and tried to appear like I was looking at something behind his head, but he saw through me and said, "Hey you. Who're you staring at, Foster?"

"Nobody," I said, and gulped at my beer.

"You calling me a nobody?"

"Look," Darrow said, coming up to me and putting a heavy hand on my shoulder. "We don't want any trouble. So you'd better come with us." When George and Darrow gave you an invitation, you didn't ever exactly feel like you could refuse, so I went with them and lived to tell the tale, and that's why I had to know the whole story. I had to see my own place in it because of what destiny had in store for me that night. It was like God had meant for someone to know the whole story, and that someone was me. Don't ask me why. The point is that I was with them as they walked out of the bar, and George put his arm around his brother and said, "Are you thinking what I'm thinking?"

"Since when have you thought anything I wasn't?"

"Since no time that I remember, buddy. Never was a pair like us. Folks'll be talking about us for years and years."

We drove out to the river crossing and they parked their pickup. I didn't say anything for fear of saying the wrong thing. "That's one dead man," Darrow said, and tossed his beer.

"That's two," George said, and tossed his.

"That's three if you count Stanley. Can't forget ol' lonesome Stanley."

"Hey, I wonder what he was thinking before that train hit him."

"Probably thought it was a spotlight."

"Yeah, he probably started to sing. He's probably still wondering how come no one's applauding."

"Train sound kinda sounds like applause. Always kinda thought a diesel engine sounded like applause."

"Naw. The rain is what sounds like applause. Or the wind, sometimes, when it's in the trees."

Darrow shouted out, "Let's all have a big hand for Stanley Andrews and the Sundowners!"

They stood there in the dark and listened to the wind.

"Naw, it don't sound nothing like applause."

"Sure it does. You just gotta use your imagination."

We got to the train tracks and started walking down them, our backs to the direction a train would come. I kept glancing over my shoulder, but George and Darrow were too excited by Stanley Andrews's sudden demise to look out for another train coming along to add them to its list.

"Hey, I know it," Darrow said. He was laughing so hard he could hardly breathe. "He must have been singing a train song."

George started laughing, too, and then he started to sing, "I can settle down and be doing fine, till I hear that train coming down the line!"

"Say, did anyone ever tell you you've gotta fine country voice? You got a talent for it, I'd say."

"Well, the thought's crossed my mind." George tossed his beer into the dark. "One more dead man."

"And another," Darrow said, tossing his. "Well, I've heard about this band that's got an opening. The man who was in the band before ruined every song he ever sang. But he's dead now."

"You don't say. How'd he die?"

"Got ran over by a spotlight."

They were hysterical by this time, laughing and laughing. George started singing all the train songs he knew. Anyone listening to them could have told they were drunk and getting drunker. I sure could. But then Darrow suddenly turned serious and said, "But you know, I guess we have to be thankful to Stanley Andrews for having the good sense and—shit, why not say it?—the common decency to kill himself. I mean, I was just sick with myself after last night. I was all ready to kill him and all but I—" Darrow looked downcast and earnest and even scared. "I discovered I didn't have it in me."

"To be honest, I didn't have it in me, either," George said.

"There are only so many opportunities like that that come along in a man's life. Destiny doesn't stand there banging on the door."

"No, it doesn't, brother."

"So I guess we have to be thankful to Stanley Andrews. After letting myself down like that, not to mention letting down my dear brother—"

"It ain't all your fault, Darrow. I let you down, too, you know."

"Well, I wasn't sure I wanted to go on living."

"Me too, brother. Me too. But now we can! It's like the preacher says, we've been delivered by the guiding hand of Providence. By God, now we can get on with our lives! And you know something else, brother? People won't ever stop talking about us. We're the damn legends."

"Damn sure! That's for damn sure!"

We walked down the track a mile, two miles, three miles, straining to see in the dark. In the distance behind us, I heard the sound of an approaching train.

"Hear that?" George said.

"Sure do," Darrow said. "It's like music!"

"The lonesome whistle blow!"

"Like a good ol' country song!"

"First one to look's a Stanley Andrews!"

"You're on! First one who even moves is a Stanley Andrews!"

I stepped off the tracks a ways and watched them balancing on the rails and elbowing each other, keeping their backs to the approaching train—and I guess those two boys were right about folks never forgetting them. You can't even mention the legendary Stanley Andrews without bringing them up, the late great George and Darrow Drumlin. I think maybe they knew this, too, because they laughed, you know. I was there as a witness, and I'm telling you that they laughed and laughed, probably because they could feel the rails vibrating and tickling their feet as the train moved toward them. They thought this was funny. They thought everything was funny. The trees were funny and the wind was funny and the spotlight of a moon was the biggest joke of all. But most of all they laughed at how the train light cast their shadows across the tracks and even up into the trees, making them look so tall, you might have even thought that they were already legends.

Hideout

WHEN HE COMES out of his house, he sees his ragged winter tree decorated by painted shoes, red and purple, blue and green, hanging by their laces. A little Christmas tinsel clings to the limbs, fluttering in the wind. His neighborhood boys mean to torment him, but they cannot realize how much pleasure he takes in this, his tree mummified in tissue paper, providing a nest for a mailbox, a wooden chair, a battalion of colored balloons that dangle and bob from the branches. There are birds there, too, sometimes. Grackles and finches.

In the spring, the boys gather outside his house at night. They giggle from his lilac bushes. Their laughter baits him, pulling him out of his sleep. He comes out on his porch, keeping in the shadows. He sits in an old weathered rocking chair for an hour, for two hours, as if he is trying to hide but knowing they can see him. His timing is perfect. Just when he feels that they are growing bored, he rises suddenly from his chair, giving the appearance of one scanning the darkness. He is a hunter. They are his prey. Their bodies grow tense, their laughter more restrained. As he steps off his porch, they struggle to get their feet beneath them, much like cats do when they are getting ready to spring, and then he breaks his silence—"You, kids!"—and they scatter in all directions, maybe six or seven or eight of them.

For hours afterward, he patrols his block as quietly as he can, as familiar with the shadows and the hiding places as they are. He comes up behind them, giving a grunt, giving fair warning, and they are off again like rabbits from an open hutch. When winter comes, the game is discontinued for the year, although sometimes, even in winter, the sun bright and the air cold, they adorn his bare trees or scatter bright green bottles or sign their nicknames, their animal names, in piss in the snow. Sometimes he finds a frost print, a nose pressed against a window. Sometimes he finds their little tracks go to the edge of his lawn and then vanish in a flutter of prints that remind him of wings. In the spring, they all continue the game again, except it is a different pack, some having grown up, some having become bored. Only a few lag behind to pass on their tricks.

He does not know any boy by his name. Individually, they do not matter. They replenish themselves. They are always alike, one year to another. And no one has ever come to harm by this. How could he hurt them? There is a cord between them. He depends upon them as they do upon him. Their fear of him is necessary, because he makes their secret hiding places safe. Through them, he has come to know that growing old is only make-believe. He hears them laughing. They draw him out of his house, his screen door slamming, his heart pounding as he searches for them, crouching low in his bushes, feeling safe for that moment and trying not to breathe.

Demon in the Closet

MOM WAS STANDING at the closet door, holding her face in her hands like it'd fall off if she didn't hold it there. I've seen this look before, and it always meant something bad. Like she was remembering every bad thing we ever did, so we all tried to act dumb. "All I want to know," she finally said, "is which one of you brought that thing in here!" We'd been hanging out in the house all day, and who knows what we'd done wrong by then. Could have been a thousand things, so while Mom went back into the kitchen to fix herself a drink, we all snuck over to the closet to take a look, and there it was, a demon, and a gray one, too. Gray as mud and hiding there, all folded up and afraid.

"Not me," Regan said. "I didn't do it." And Virgil said, "Don't blame me."

At first, I thought it was just another overcoat, one that nobody ever used anymore and practically forgot about. It was trying to hide between Dad's Sunday coat and Virgil's coveralls, staring at us sideways, looking like it'd like to hide. I mean it was flat. Like there should have been a hanger sticking up out of its neck.

"Morgana?" Mom said. At the sound of my name, that demon started thrashing around.

"It wasn't me," I said.

"Well, don't try to tell me that it got there on its own!"

I didn't see why that was so impossible. Maybe it crawled out of the toilet, for all I knew. Or maybe one of us brought it in and forgot about it. It wouldn't have been the first time something like that happened.

Mom stood there, rattling the ice in her glass and narrowing her eyes at us, and said, "You wait until your Dad gets home. We are not a family who hides things," and I knew that the blame that's been coming my way since the day I was born was going to get to me soon.

Regan and Virgil hung around the kitchen helping Mom, trying to pretend they were on her side in this, so I went back into my room and practically crawled into the closet myself. I thought I could hear something scuffling in the walls and ceiling. I thought about the time a raccoon got under the roof, and the time birds flew down the stovepipe, and how one time we came home and found a stray cat, all green-eyed and scared, how it banged into walls and doors so hard while it was trying to get out that it hurt itself. That cat had a fit or something in the kitchen and Dad took it somewheres. I thought about that cat a lot, considering how short a time we had it. A black and orange Halloween cat with long matted hair. In fact, we didn't even get it named until long after we knew for certain it was dead.

Soon enough, I heard Dad come home and Mom called, "Supper!" I went out into the kitchen where Virgil and Regan glared at me and Mom dished it out, noodles and goop, and Dad sat there in a trance, chewing his food, so I knew she hadn't told him about the demon yet. When Dad's eating, he gets real dreamy, and you can get away with murder almost, as long as you're fairly quiet about it, so after I stirred my food up and faked a few bites, I snuck off for another look in the closet. A little light shined in on the demon's eye, and he opened it a little. He'd been sleeping. I was almost sorry to wake him. His eye looked exactly like a dog's eye to me, real round and sad, blinking and filling up with tears like he was starting to cry. We've never had a dog, except the stray Regan and I hid for a while. Mom and Dad never knew about that, though, and that stray was so mangled up in fur that it didn't really give you a fair idea of what a dog looks like, either. It hung itself on a leash before we got to know him. But I've seen this dog kind of thing at other people's places. And that's how that demon looked.

Dad was starting to come to, so I shut the door real quick. I knew that if Dad ever found out about that demon he'd take him out some place in the country and we'd never see him again. So I held my breath as Dad moved to the living room, right across from the closet where the demon was hiding, and started smoking his pipe. That was a good thing, because I knew Mom would have about ten minutes to get out the truth about the demon before her eyes started swelling shut. It always went that way. She'd have something to say, and he'd smoke her out. So I stood there guarding the closet door all evening, and if Dad wanted slippers, I got him slippers, and if he wanted a blanket, I got him a blanket, and that demon was real good about keeping itself a secret. Finally, Mom went into a sneezing fit, taking her drink downstairs, and Dad was dumb with tobacco and was about ready for bed, blinking his eyes and jerking his head back up. But just then, when I thought everything was going to turn out fine, that's when Tony showed up with his girlfriend, Alice.

"Go tell your mother Tony's here," Dad said, awake again and nervous. Mom came upstairs, and she took Tony's coat. She looked real tired. We watched her hang it up in the closet like it wasn't anything unusual. Everyone was acting like Tony just brought home the flu. I noticed that Virgil was trying hard not to breathe, and then Mom sneezed again. Alice said, "Gesundheit!" and I heard the demon shift around in the closet, I suppose trying to get comfortable. But later on I learned that word, whatever it means anyway, does things to demons. They get bothered and shift around. They don't like loud noises, either.

"Well, we're staying over tonight," Tony finally said.

I watched Dad bite his pipe and puff while Virgil stared at Dad like he wanted Dad to puff and blow up. Virgil told us once that one of these times when Dad's smoking up the house he's going to bring him a cup of gasoline instead of his tea.

After a long quiet time Dad said, "All right. But if you're in my house you have to live by my rules." He said that because Tony and Alice weren't married yet, and one time Dad caught Alice and Tony in bed together, and the whole time he screamed at them, Alice bawled and Tony hid under the covers.

Tony said, "So is that okay?"

Dad said, "That's just fine. Tony can sleep in Virgil's room, and Alice?" Alice jerked her head up and looked at him, scared. "You can sleep on the couch."

I guess I kind of panicked when Dad said that because I didn't want Alice out where she could get in that closet. I said, "I can sleep on the couch. Alice can sleep with Regan." Alice said, "Oh, I wouldn't want to impose," looking scared, but Regan said, "I don't mind," and I said, "I like the couch anyway." And Regan really started to smile at Alice and said, "We could have fun," but Alice said, "Oh no, oh no, I couldn't," and she really looked scared, like we were going to make her sleep with Regan no matter what she said.

Dad started to scream, "Didn't you *hear* me? I said Alice will be sleeping out here on the couch!" and that settled it. He watched and made sure that we pulled out blankets and sheets from the closet and that we made up the couch for Alice. He would have watched and made sure Alice undressed and got between those covers, too, but Tony'd already gone to bed, and so Dad did, too. When we turned the lights off on her, Alice was sitting there on the couch with her coat still on, as though she wanted to be ready to leave at any moment.

❀　❀　❀

I was pretty tired from all that stress and all, so I slipped into my pajamas and climbed into bed with Regan. "Mom will probably tell Dad tomorrow," Regan said, like she was making excuses for her. "He was so tired tonight, and you know how he gets when he's tired." Regan wanted to sit up and talk about the demon and where it came from and what it meant, but I wasn't much interested because all I wanted was a good night's rest. I didn't get it, though. In the middle of the night, Regan pushed my shoulder. I checked to see if I'd crossed the line in the middle of the bed, but I hadn't. Then she whispered in my ear that she could hear someone walking around. "Who is it?" I said, and she listened for a while and whispered, "It's Tony. He's going out to get at Alice."

She didn't have to tell me any more. From then on, I could hear for myself. Alice said Tony's name, and then after they'd shifted each other around on the couch, I could hear her say his name over and over, and everything got louder and louder, and about two minutes later we heard Dad get up, real fast, and charge into the living room, and we jumped out of bed just in time to see Dad grabbing onto Tony by one foot and dragging him off her. Tony was screaming and trying to kick at Dad with his other foot, and I could see Virgil peeking out from behind the curtain watching the whole thing. Alice was covered to her neck with blankets and screaming, probably thinking that Dad was going to kill him, and Tony was trying to cover his thing up, but it was pretty shrunken up anyway by now, by fright I guess. Pretty soon the demon got scared, too, and started banging around in the closet, which nobody but us kids could hear because of all the noise, and all this was happening in the dark, so I knew I had to stop it before someone broke a leg, so I turned on the light.

The light shocked them, all right. Alice and Tony and Dad just froze, but that demon still thumped around for a while like he was trying to claw through the back wall and get away. Not only that, but Dad and Tony and Alice all heard it. Dad dropped Tony's foot. "What's that?" he said. Tony scrambled away toward Alice and tore at her covers, and I thought he was going to try to get at her again, but they were fighting over blankets, naked and ashamed like they were. Dad asked us, "Did you hear anything in that closet?" and Tony said, "I heard something, Dad," turning all agreeable. I knew that this was going to be blamed on me. "Did you hear that, Alice?" Dad asked her. "Yes, sir," she said, real agreeable, too. "Mom?" Dad said.

Mom had just come into the room, and really tired-looking, she walked up to the closet and opened the door, and we all kind of jumped back, Dad most of all. Mom said, "Why don't you look for yourself?" I don't know, maybe she hoped that that demon would scare Dad to death. Maybe she thought he'd stiffen up and fall right on his back, but that wasn't what happened. Dad crept toward the door, slow and ready for anything, and he started paging through the clothes, like he was picking out something to wear. For a while, I thought nothing was going to come of it. I thought he might overlook that demon, but then he must have seen it finally, because he started to shout, "Hey! You! What the hell are you doing in there? Hey, you, get out of there!"

Dad started pushing away clothes and hangers, digging through the closet to get at the demon, screaming at that poor thing the whole time. When he got ahold of it, he dragged it out into the living room where he wrestled with the demon on the living room rug, but it didn't take that long before Dad had one of its paws behind its back with one hand, and a good grip on its ear with the other, and he was grinding the side of the demon's face into the carpet. I squatted down and took a look at its face. That demon didn't even have a mouth. It just looked at me, really sorry, and breathed through its nose.

"Somebody get me a rope," Dad said. Tony jumped to help. He got some cord for a clothesline out of the basement, and before long Dad had the demon tied up to a chair. Dad wrapped the extra cord about the part of its body where its peter or woo should've been, and we didn't have time to see which it had, but it didn't look like it had anything at all. And then Dad started screaming, "Who brought this thing in here?" but nobody had an answer for him.

"All I brought in here was Alice," Tony said, miserable and still mostly naked.

Dad turned on Mom. "Did you?" But she stared back at him and kept staring. We couldn't believe it. It was like the first time she ever stood up to him. It was weird. Meanwhile, the demon blinked right at me. It looked right at me, and it only struggled and shivered every once in a while. "It wouldn't be here unless someone sinned," Regan said. Dad's eyes locked on me, too, since he couldn't get the best of Mom. "Go get a Bible," Mom said, and off Regan went. You could tell it was driving the demon crazy to be all tied up. It gave a big shake like a fish does, and it really started to fight those ropes, so I knew that Dad hadn't hurt it too bad. But then it started staring at me again, and Virgil asked, "How come that demon keeps staring at you?" and I shouted out, "How should I know! Just leave me alone!" But the demon was *still* staring at me, so I screamed at the demon, "Quit it! Cut it out!" Finally the demon looked whipped and stared at the floor. I felt mean to put that demon in its place, but staring at someone who doesn't want to be stared at is a terrible thing to do, not to mention rude.

When Regan came back with the Bible, Dad started to look pretty worried. Mom paged around and finally found the part about how Jesus drove the demons out of a man's body and how Jesus forced the demons on a bunch of pigs, and they screamed and went crazy and drowned themselves. Regan nodded her head and said that the story was true, it really happened. Like she was an eyewitness. Then Mom read that same story a second time, only this time she read it right into the demon's ear. I wouldn't do that to nobody, but I thought the demon took it pretty well. He hung his head down low, but he kept his pride. It wasn't like he disappeared or anything. Mom pointed a finger at the demon. "It's in the name of Jesus Christ that I order you to get out of here!" She might have been drunk again, I don't know. Dad said, "What the hell are you trying to do, Mom?" She said something about "driving the demon out of our mists," and Dad said, "Well, it ain't working, and you're starting to scare me."

"Maybe it would help if we'd loosen the cords a bit," Tony said. "Maybe he'll walk away." But Dad said, "You hold it right there, boy. You keep that demon tied up." Right away Alice wanted us to call the police or at least a priest, but Dad said, "They're the last people I want to know about this." I've never seen Dad look so guilty. I felt kind of guilty, too, because that demon was still staring at me. I guess he thought this whole thing was my fault. "So what do we do with it?" Alice asked, and Tony said, "Just get rid of it, I suppose." Alice flinched and turned her head. We tried talking about it, but no one had any ideas except Regan, who said that maybe we should take it to the animal shelter, but Virgil started to cry when she said that, because he's always wanted a dog, and Dad would never let him. "Maybe we should put it up for adoption," Alice said. Leave it to Alice to be so stupid. We all made faces at each other and didn't even care if Alice saw them or not, but Mom actually took Alice seriously and said, "Adoption?" She sat down next to Alice on the couch and put her arm around her, comforting her. And pretty soon Alice was starting to cry. Mom said to her, "You can tell me the truth, sweetie," and then, "You're not pregnant, are you?" How Mom knew this I'll never figure out, but Alice started to blubber and bob her head yes. Tony sat on the couch and looked down at his naked knees.

"I don't want it," Alice said. I saw that demon's eye tear over as if he knew what it was like being an unwanted child. Tony always said the last three of us were accidents. He was the last one the folks wanted. "You're not going to give it up, are you?" Mom asked. Alice shrugged, while Tony started talking about how that made the most sense. Dad screamed, "You're not going to give away my grandchild!" and made like he was going to hit Tony, but that demon started to choke and flinch so pitifully that everyone's attention was naturally drawn to it. I saw the demon work around its jaw as if it was trying to say something, and I wondered why God would give a demon a jaw but not a mouth to open it with. And Mom was telling Alice, "I'll help you take care of it, dear," like Alice was going to be having a puppy or something.

Dad started getting right in Tony's face. "You mean you were trying to get at that poor girl even when she was carrying your child? I never did that to your mother!" It was like the sickest thing Dad ever heard, but I could see from the way Tony was moving inside the blanket that even feeling guilty about trying to get at Alice made him feel excited again. I could see that Tony was thinking about what she looked like when he looked under her blanket. And Mom and Dad and Tony argued back and forth for about an hour before we all noticed that the demon dropped off to sleep. Sleep seemed pretty sensible at that point, so then we all went off to bed, too, too tired to think. Considering everything that happened, the folks thought it was okay to put Tony and Alice in Virgil's room. They moved Virgil in bed with Regan and me, and we all settled in for the night, but I didn't really sleep that well, because I was afraid Virgil was going to pee all over me.

Once Dad tried to cure Virgil by buying some kind of bedsheet all strung through with wires. It was hooked up to a flashing light and an alarm, but Virgil only got worse. Every night Dad had to stumble through the dark toward Virgil's room to hit the off switch. And one night instead of hitting the off switch Dad was so mad that he yanked apart the cord, and the thing stopped working after that. Virgil hasn't wet his bed in a year, but sometimes Mom gets worried that he doesn't go to the bathroom at all, so she stands him in there and makes him do it while she watches. But I didn't trust him one inch. I kept my hand close to his thing, so I'd have early warning and time to jump up. I was in the middle, too, and Regan forgot that Virgil was there and kept kicking me for being on her side of the bed. She'd shove me back to Virgil's side, and finally I held my breath and tried to make myself thin, and then I was floating and happy, and warm, too, and then I woke up, and my butt was wet. I took a shower and put on clean pajamas and went out to the living room to sleep on the couch, but I didn't sleep that well because I got real worried about the demon. All that demon had to breathe through was its nose, and sometimes the nose stopped up, and the demon stopped breathing and panicked and snorted. He didn't wake up because I guess he was used to it. So I finally got used to it too. I listened to it snore and watched it for a while and kind of wished I could talk to the demon, and then I fell asleep.

❀   ❀   ❀

When I woke up in the morning Mom was vacuuming around the demon's chair, and that demon was pretty scared about it because she was bumping his feet and being kind of rough about it. Then she raced off with the vacuum into the kitchen with the power cord trailing behind her. Even though it was past time for Dad to go to work, he came walking in the living room with his pipe and a newspaper and a cup of tea. Virgil was tagging along, real anxious looking, and I thought I could smell gasoline. But Dad sipped without making a face and sat down in his chair and started reading, ignoring all of us. Regan was practically sitting on my feet, I don't know for how long.

"We don't have to go to school," Regan said. Mom came racing back with the vacuum like she was doing laps. Dad screamed at her, "Will you turn that thing off!" The machine died down. Tony and Alice drug their butts into the living room looking like they hadn't slept at all. "Move your legs," Tony said to me, and he and Alice sat down on the couch between me and Regan. Finally Virgil came out dragging a garbage bag full of paper towels and said, "Can someone help me move the bed outside?"

The mattress got stuck in a couple doors, but we managed all right once Dad started helping. We put it out on the front porch to air. Tony and Dad beat it back indoors like it was poison out there, but Virgil and I stayed on the porch, kind of stunned, because it was October and a great day. All the leaves were lying on the ground like about a thousand decks of cards, but only in our yard, in nobody else's. It was the kind of cool day when you think you'll never get tired. Pretty soon Regan was out on the porch with us. Mom stuck her head out and said, "If you want to be outside then you better put some clothes on." Regan and I were still in our pajamas. The day was so great that we almost hadn't noticed. We ran back inside and dug our overalls out of the closet. I had half a mind to try to talk the folks into letting the demon come out with us, because he looked like he could use some air. He had this sad-dog I-wanna-come-along look. I felt sorry that he had to stay inside on such a nice day.

"Wait a minute," Virgil said. "Don't we have to go to school?"

"Everyone gets to stay home today," Mom said.

"Is it a holiday?" Virgil asked, and everyone thought about this for the longest time.

"By God, I think it is," Dad said. "Only I can't remember what it is."

"Well, it must be," Mom said. "There's no school today, at least I don't think there is."

"Well, if I'm staying home it has to be a holiday," Dad said. "The only other time I stay home is when I'm sick."

"So how do you feel?" Mom asked him.

"I feel fine," Dad said.

"Well, it must be a holiday, then," Mom said.

"I'm not sick at all," Dad said.

We spent a lot of time going in and out of the house that day, banging doors. Nobody screamed. Nobody told us to go away. The sky was all cracked up with bare branches, and we found plenty of things to do. After we played in the leaves, we started packing them up. I mean, we hardly even cleaned our rooms, and here we were cleaning up the whole front yard. We had so much energy we could have packed up the whole neighborhood if we wanted to. We even found time to stare about and blink at how different the yard looked. We all felt good, even Virgil. "Sometimes wetting the bed feels good," he said, and it kind of made sense. All of a sudden I kind of liked Virgil, so I pushed him into a pile of leaves. He didn't even cry.

When we went inside Mom was still cleaning, so we all joined in. Even Dad. We opened up the windows and doors because it was our last chance to air the place out before winter shut us up for good. We helped make supper. We set the table. We even talked about what the demon should eat, or whether he didn't need to since he didn't have a mouth. Virgil set a place for the demon at the table and scooted him up to it. We all laughed about that, even Dad, even Alice and Mom and Tony. If that demon had a mouth, it would have laughed, too. I think Dad even said grace that night, but I can't remember what we had to eat because of what happened next, because there was a knock on the door.

Everybody got really tense. Mom whispered to Dad, "Should I answer it?" Dad looked scared. Another knock. Before anyone could stop him, Virgil jumped up and ran to the door. He looked out the little fish-eye and screamed, "I knew it, I knew it!" Dad tried to grab him but too late. Virgil had already pulled the door open, and a witch, a ghost, a zombie, and a princess walked into the living room. They held up their bags.

"I knew it," Virgil said, starting to cry. He whined, "Mom! Mom!" over and over, blaming the whole thing on her. "Mom! I'm missing Halloween!"

Mom panicked and screamed, "Someone go find Virgil a costume!"

"Virgil can't come with us," the princess said.

Virgil screamed at this princess to shut up and continued crying. Mom screamed, "Someone run to the store and pick up some treats!" Dad brushed past the trick-or-treaters as if he were answering an emergency, and I guess he was, and he was glad to be needed.

"You mean you don't have any treats for us?" the princess asked.

"No treats?" the ghost said, almost happy about it.

Then the zombie started chanting "Trick! Trick!" and so did the rest of them. The ghost screamed, "Slash their tires! Soap their windows!"

"Wait!" Mom said in a panic. "Wait, I—I have something for you!" She went out into the kitchen and got four red potatoes and dropped one in each bag. The kids stared at those potatoes like they couldn't believe it. Even I couldn't believe it. "Now, run," Mom said, "before it gets dark and the devil gets you!" But they weren't afraid of us at all, and they went outside yelling "Trick! Trick!" and about fifteen minutes later those four red potatoes came crashing through Virgil's bedroom window. Virgil was with Regan and me in our bedroom, though, and so he didn't know how mean these kids were. We were putting dresses on him because that's all we could think of. And he came running out before we even zipped him up.

"Are they still here?" Virgil said, meaning the other kids.

"They've gone ahead, dear," Mom said. Virgil ran to the door. "Wait!" he screamed, starting to run out after them just as Dad was coming back up the walk. "Hold it, boy," Dad said. "You're not going out looking like that!" So we went back and cut holes in a sheet and tied knots all over it. Virgil was either a ghost or a white spider. We sent him out with the next group of kids who came around, and then more kids came. Dad and Mom were really enjoying the costumes and all, once they had candy enough for everyone and the panic was over. I was kind of proud of them because they were real generous with the candy, but then it got weird, and I was kind of embarrassed by Dad.

One time when a group of really little kids came by and yelled "Trick or treat," Dad said, "Okay. I'll take a trick. Who will perform a trick for me? Stand on your head! Turn a somersault!" Then he got down on his hands and knees so he'd be on those little kids' level, so he wouldn't scare them he said, and tried to show them how. Soon little fairies and cat-people and little Batmans and witches were all rolling around on our living room rug, getting their feet tangled up in each other's costumes. All those little kids' parents were standing behind them thinking this was real funny. Even Mom laughed. It was weird. Then Dad scooted the demon around so it was facing the living room and could see everything that was going on.

"That's some demon you got there," one of the parents said, not thinking it was real. "Where'd you get it?"

"Where was it, dear?" Dad asked Mom, almost like he was teasing her.

"The closet," she said, like she was teasing back, and the man who asked the question really laughed about that answer.

"I don't know if I could stand having a demon so lifelike in my living room. Weren't you afraid it would scare the kids?"

"Kids are tough little critters," Dad said. "Just look at them."

They were rolling around, and a couple of them were even playing with the demon's toes and looking in his ears. But when they started to play rough and actually pull on the demon's ears, Dad just said to them, "Play nice, now" a couple times, real firm but real gentle, too, and right away those kids settled down and started to pet the demon. I bet those parents were thinking that Dad was a real ace with children. The fathers who were there probably decided right then and there to play with their kids a lot more. All those people told Regan and me how well we were behaving, how helpful we were when we followed Mom into the kitchen to help her, and Dad was helping her, too.

"It must be nice to do everything as a family," one man said to us. We started to serve those people cake and coffee while Tony and Alice took their children on the rounds of the neighborhood. More trick-or-treaters came by, more parents stayed. Dad got a big gorilla suit out of the closet. I didn't even know there was a gorilla suit in there, and a good one too. Dad made a big deal out of how it wasn't "synthetic," and he put it on, and from then on he was absolutely crazy for an hour. Kids came to the door and squealed at him, and parents smiled. Right away they knew they were going to have a good time. Dad made these kids turn somersaults and did his own, drooping his arms down and hooting and scooting around the living room. Turned out that Dad knew how to do a real good gorilla. And Mom had upgraded the treats to popcorn balls. I don't know how she had time to make them.

When Dad got tired and the kids stopped coming, Mom started serving all these people whiskey and whipped cream in their coffees, and Dad stood like some kind of hero with his gorilla's head under his arm. All the other men were standing around him, remarking how well his suit was made.

"And this demon's pretty well put together, too. How do you get it to move like that?"

"Hydraulics," Dad said.

"You don't say? Where are the pipes? How's she powered?"

"It's a he," Virgil yelled, coming in the door. He managed to find a group of younger kids who didn't mind being with him, and he had a sack full of candy that Tony and Alice were sorting through to check for razor blades and thumbtacks and poison.

Dad said something about the demon being radio powered and then started talking about "solid-state construction" or something. "You won't find a single seam on that demon," Dad was saying to them. He was practically bragging and calling it "his demon" now. "If any of you men can find a demon that can match my demon, well, I'll eat my pipe," which was half eaten anyway.

When everybody started to leave, we had to hear about a hundred squealing people thank us and say they'd never had a better Halloween in their entire lives. Then when the last ghost and his parents were gone, everybody collapsed into bed, tired, but feeling good, like we deserved to go to sleep. I slept out on the couch again, with the demon sitting right there, still all tied up. When I saw how happy and comfortable the demon seemed to be even in all those ropes, I started to think that maybe the demon couldn't run away even if it wanted to. So in the middle of the night I untied it. The demon didn't even get up and stretch. It sat there. So after I saw that it was really a he, I guess, I covered him up with one of my blankets, but he didn't pay enough attention to it, so it kept slipping off. I got tired real fast of trying to keep him covered up, so I lay on the couch and managed to ignore him. Every time I opened my eyes he was blinking and staring at me, and the next thing I knew it was Sunday morning.

❀   ❀   ❀

When we got up that morning, Regan started in with getting us to go to church. Regan once read the Bible cover to cover, but of course it took a few false starts before she could make it past all the rapes and murders and sodomites and Gomorrahs and husbands and wives acting like brothers and sisters. She said there was even these two women who got their father drunk so they could have his children. "And that was only by page 20," Regan said. "I still had more than a thousand pages to go!"

But Regan's nothing if not stubborn. She got through that Bible, and this morning she was bound and determined to get us into church. The first I knew of it was when Mom came in and screamed at me to put on a dress. I never wear a dress 'cause it makes my clothes feel like they have no bottom to them, but everyone else was already dressed. Regan had on white gloves, and Virgil had an oversized sport jacket that covered his shorts so it looked like he didn't have pants on at all. Even Dad had a suit on him, only it was kind of short in the arms, and I'd never noticed before how hairy and long Dad's arms looked.

Anyway, after we tied the demon back up and put him back in the closet, we drove off looking for a church. We just drove around until we found one open, and even though we were late, we walked right up to the front where there was nobody except this old woman, dressed all in black and creaking in her pew. Everyone else seemed to be sitting in the back, like they were afraid of something up there in the front of the church. We didn't even know what religion it was, either, but whatever it was, it was dying out. I've never seen so many old people dying in one place. They were small and hunched over and tired looking, like they'd been dragged this way too many times.

The pastor was in the middle of his sermon, stammering and fumbling at his book and saying something about, "He who receives me— excuse me. He who receives you who receives him—who receives me receives him—him who. Excuse me, he who, he who receives me who, who receives you, receives him who receives you." And then he slouched over like he'd never get it right, but Regan tensed up, like this was some really important message. She started paging around in her Bible, making those pages go lick, lick, lick, lick, and the pastor noticed her and started getting more nervous. For a while both of them were going at it, paging through their Bibles like they were in a race, but finally the pastor seemed to come on something halfway familiar to him and said, "Our Bible verse for today is 'And Jesus sternly caged them, "See that no one knocks it. . . ."'" But then he was back to staring at his book again, like it wasn't saying quite what he thought it would.

Finally Regan had to step in. She stood up. "Just where is that?" She sat down. He blinked at us like he heard a pew speak. "Matthew," he said. Regan stood up again. "Matthew what?" She sat down. He looked at his watch and then at the page and said, "Well, I'd say it's 9:30." I swear, it was like they were talking in code. I couldn't follow any of this, but right off Regan paged to some spot in the Bible like she wasn't too far off to begin with. She read a bit and then said to him, "Keep reading." The pastor stared at her like he was shocked out of his mind, like no one ever told him what to do. But that didn't bother Regan any. She just said, "Read on, read the next part, too."

It took the pastor some time to find out where he was again, but then he started reading in this tired voice: "As they were going away, behold, a dumb demoniac was brought to him. And when the demon had been cast out, the dumb man spoke." I looked at the Bible on Regan's lap and couldn't believe it, "dumb demoniac" was what it said, only the pastor didn't get to read on to tell us what the dumb man had to say because Regan butted in.

She asked, "Do you believe in demons?"

It took him a long time to understand the question. Behind me, all those old people were staring right at the pastor like dogs. You know what I mean. All there, and eyes not moving a bit. When a dog looks at you, you know it. I don't even think they were blinking.

That pastor started to grip and grab his own hands. He acted scared, put on the spot. Really nervous. You could tell he was going through his head and coming up with blanks, and then he started paging around in the Bible, and then he just stood there with his eyes closed.

"In those days people thought . . . diseases of the mind . . . were caused by demons." Maybe he was thinking up something he studied in school, or maybe he was making this up, I couldn't tell.

"So you don't believe in demons," Regan said.

"No, oh no, not in demons." He seemed a little relieved to be able to admit this.

"Jesus believed in demons," Regan said. "Do you believe in Jesus?"

"Why, of course, child."

"Even demons believe in Jesus."

"Yes, but—"

"They believe in God, too."

"If there were demons, child, I'm sure they'd believe in God. It says in James 'even the demons believe—and shudder.'" And then he started talking louder, as if he were talking to all of us, trying to make a sermon out of it: "Demoniacs, epileptics, paralytics . . . all these were classified together because they were mysterious. . . . They involved fits and seizures . . . mental pain and anguish and confusion." He started rubbing his eyes something fierce and didn't say anything else, so I guessed he thought he was finished.

"Jesus cast out the *demons*," Regan said, almost shouting. "That's what he called them, and that's what he believed. I believe whatever Jesus believed." And there was a rumble from the old people sitting in back, and the pastor looked up, halfway surprised. There's a lot that's ugly about a crowd of people getting angry. They were siding in with Regan. The pastor knew it, too. Maybe they were tired of his always trying to be better than them, I don't know. Maybe they were giving up on heaven and everything, not seeing what difference it made anyhow. All I knew was that pastor had trouble on his hands, and he knew it.

Mom looked proud enough to bust her seams. "Do you believe in the Devil?" Regan demanded. The pastor tried to smile, but his attempt just looked scary. He was trying to make friends with her, I could tell, but it didn't help. "The Devil's a different story, child," he said.

"Do you believe in the Devil, sir?"

"Yes, of course I do," he said, real quick. He looked out over his church and tried to get control of it. People were standing up in back and shaking their fists at him, but they were too old to make much noise. It was like they were screaming at him from a long way off. "I believe," he said, looking scared. He was gripping and grabbing at his own hands again and said, "Let us bow our heads in prayer. . . . I believe

in God the Father Almighty and in Jesus Christ his only Son our Lord."
A few people joined with the prayer but gave up when the pastor lost
confidence and his voice faded out, and then everyone started yelling at
once. I've never seen Mom so happy in her life. She and Regan were
shouting and testifying about their sin and everyone else's, while Dad,
Tony, and Alice slumped down in the pew. Virgil stared at Mom and
kind of shivered.

"Jesus cast out demons," Regan yelled to the old people in back.
"Does this man cast out demons?"

"No!" an old woman yelled, happy, like she'd been waiting for this.

"But I'm not Jesus," the pastor whined.

"You certainly aren't," Mom said, outraged that he'd even think he
could be.

Regan was mocking him by now. "Jesus believed in demons, but you
don't, do you? Because you're too good. Because you think Jesus was
just a superstitious old fool, don't you?"

"He thinks he's better than everyone," an old woman yelled. Dad
was trying to get us to leave. I wanted to and Alice and Tony wanted to,
but Virgil stayed behind with Mom and Regan. He hugged Mom and
she hugged him back, and then he stumbled backward into the aisle.

"I'm possessed!" Virgil yelled out. He was shaking in a fit. "I got a
demon in me!" He fell down, right there on the carpet, and all those old
people stared at that pastor like all this was his fault for ignoring demons
all this time. I swear those old people started crawling out of their pews
and limping and hobbling down the aisles, coughing and growling, and
that stupid old pastor kept saying, "You may be seated," like he was giving them permission to sit down after saying some prayer. Only they
kept coming. Dad grabbed Virgil by the foot and drug him out of the
church, even pushing some of those old people down, but that still
didn't stop them. They kept coming. When they finally got that pastor
trapped in a corner, I had to feel sorry for him, but what could we do?
We'd already done pretty much all we could, so we all took off, and the
last thing I saw of that church was a big hump of people piling on each
other in front of the altar, with Jesus hanging on a big cross right over
their heads, looking skinny and sad, like he wanted to be someplace else.

❊   ❊   ❊

"Bet you he's not there," Regan said to me when we got back home, so
we bet on it. We bet everything we had, and we spat in our hands and
shook them, and when we opened the closet that demon was gone! But
then we heard some scampering down the hall, and we caught that
demon in Virgil's room, trying to get under the bed, so Dad grabbed the

demon by his foot and dragged him out into the living room, while the demon tried to snag the carpet going down the hall. The demon didn't fight, though, once they got it back into that chair. He let them put the ropes back, even. He didn't mind. Long as nobody screamed at him.

"All right!" Mom shouted, looking right at Dad. "I've had enough. I want to know right now who brought that thing in here!"

"It was Morgana!" Regan yelled, and the demon thrashed around at the sound of my name, which I would have appreciated that demon not doing.

"Sure wasn't me," Dad said.

"So how do I know that?" Mom said. "How do I know what you're bringing in here?"

"Well, how the hell do I know what you're doing around here all alone all day, bitch!" Dad screamed, and Regan said, "Uh-oh." He said that word. That word mother doesn't like and, oh, Mom slapped him hard, let me tell you. But right away she looked sorry that she did. I guess her hand got away from her.

"I'm sorry, dear," she said. She looked scared and shut her eyes like she was starting to pray, and Dad's hand swung back. The demon and mother flinched right at the same time. I covered my mouth, and Regan dropped her Bible and covered her ears, and Dad's hand flew back so fast that I saw it in three places at once, and Dad swung his arm as hard as he could and cracked the demon's nose. Crunched it. That nose lay flat against the side of the demon's face, and its face went all droopy like Grandpa's did when he had the stroke. Dad stepped back, shocked with himself. The demon started twitching around inside his ropes, dreadfully in pain. Dad started saying, "Oh shit" and "Oh no, oh no, oh no!" He ran up to the demon and, with his hands trembling, held the demon's nose back in place, but that nose was only an empty sock now. Dad had knocked all the bone right out of it.

"Tony, Tony, my God, do something!"

"Do what?"

"I don't know! Get me some tape!"

Dad's hands were shaking as he fumbled at the demon's nose. I guess he thought that if he held it in place long enough, it'd stay.

"What kind of tape?"

"Something sticky," Dad said. "Something like duct tape. Anything."

Tony ran off and came back with a sticky black mass of something more like flypaper than anything. Soon Dad taped a cross of tape across the demon's face while I yelled, "Don't close off his nose!" but Dad glared at me, just to tell me blame was coming back in my direction if I didn't shut up. After that he turned on Mom, pointing his finger right at her throat. "If you hit me again, woman," but she did it anyway. She got him right on the nose this time. Then Alice got sick, and Tony went into the bathroom to help her, and Virgil went back into his room and crawled under the covers and did that thing he does when Mom and Dad are screaming, and Regan started to read from the Bible, and in the commotion, the demon had gotten out of his ropes again and crawled back into the closet, tearing up almost all our winter coats in the process. I don't know why he had to do something like that. I guess he was scared. He was wedged into a corner and all those shreds of blankets and coats and snowsuits and sleeping bags were lying on top of him. Mom dragged him out of there, hitting him the whole time.

"Don't hit his nose!" I yelled out. "Stop hitting his nose!" It wasn't like she was trying to. She was generally aiming at his ears but ended up catching his nose a few times, anyway. She had a funny look on her face, like something was hurting her. She might have broken her hand for how hard she was hitting him with it. She looked sick, like she wanted to stop beating the demon but couldn't. Then Regan and Virgil joined in, whipping the demon like they couldn't help themselves, either.

Look, I didn't want to be on Tony and Dad's side, but I was. Tony and Dad were just meaning to protect something they thought they owned now. They pushed Virgil and Regan and Mom away from the demon, and I mean they were rough. Tony pushed Virgil so hard that Virgil bumped his head on a doorknob, and Mom tore into Tony, and Dad grabbed Mom from behind, and Virgil grabbed hold of Tony's thigh and started biting him. Tony kicked his leg like he was trying to get rid of a dog that liked him too much, and then he started screaming, loud, because Virgil's head was snagged between Tony's legs. Dad grabbed Virgil's head like he meant to twist it off, and then Dad jumped around like a mule with a bobcat on its back, only it was Mom, digging into him. Regan kept beating on the demon. I tried to hug her around her arms, but she stomped on my foot until I let her go, and then she was right after that demon again, who was rolling around on the floor trying to cover himself up.

But then all at once that demon was on his feet, looking scared and dangerous, with a lot of energy, like he was a cornered animal. I mean, we thought he was cornered all along, being in the closet and all, being tied up. We thought that was the worst he could get. But maybe now, for the first time, he was really afraid of dying. I noticed he had cat's claws, never saw them before, and he slid them out of his paws. They were like big needles, only curved, about four or five inches long. The demon was making slow motions through the air with those needles, kind of like he was dog-paddling in water, so I let Regan go so she could get out of the demon's way, because the demon was making a lot of noise, but he couldn't growl, having no mouth. He could only snivel and snore with his nose, which was plugged up by duct tape and a lot of gray-purple blood. He sounded like he was blowing into his pop with a straw. And he was trying to wipe his nose like any human would, with his hand, and getting fed up with his nose, looking crossed-eyed at it with all that duct tape and blood and whatever. For a while he forgot about us and got mad at that nose. He wiped and sniffed and wiped and sniffed and finally reached up with one paw and picked the whole thing off, all the duct tape and the nose, too. There was just a hole there. And the demon started breathing real deep and healthy. His neck and chest seemed to grow bigger with each breath.

Dad was the first one the demon went after. The demon tried to scratch Dad a couple times, and Dad jumped around and shrieked like there was something crawly in his pants. Maybe the demon just wanted to scare him, I don't know. If that demon really wanted to scratch Dad, I'm sure he would have, and everything might have been okay if Dad hadn't tried pushing Alice in front of him, and the demon accidentally scratched her. It wasn't that big of a scratch. If the demon had been serious, he would have sliced her whole arm off, I'm sure. "You bastard!" Mom yelled. Already Alice was sitting on the floor, starting to sweat, starting to moan. I actually think that demon had a lot of sympathy for her and was sorry he got her instead of Dad, because he fell down and started to roll around on the carpet and moan himself, like he was crazy with guilt. Right away the scratch started turning red and ugly and swelling up. Alice was sweating through her clothes, and that demon started to sweat and pant through his nose socket and bloat up. He started crawling back into the closet like it was the place he most wanted to die.

"You bastard, look what you've done," Mom yelled at the demon. But I don't think the demon was well enough to be able to hear her. It was like he was in a fever or something. And he couldn't draw his claws back in, so he had a terrible time getting hold of the doorknob. I could tell this ticked off Dad something fierce, because he'd sanded and varnished all the woodwork last winter. The demon tried to pull himself to his feet by grabbing the curtains, but they turned to shreds. He tried to scratch his way up the wallpaper, but that came off like rotten bark on a rotten tree. I don't know if that demon was crying or choking, but he was doing something. He was trying to hold his own throat only like I say he couldn't get his claws back in so I was afraid he was going to poke his eyes out.

"Oh my God," Alice started crying, on her back with her knees sticking up, "My God, my God, he's leaving me, he's leaving me now!"

"Who, Tony?" Dad asked.

"She's having a miscarriage!" Mom screamed, loud enough to be heard above Alice's howling. And Alice howled something fierce. I guess a bunch of our neighbors came out of their houses at that point and looked around, but the sound was too wild, and they couldn't tell where it was coming from. I don't know why they hadn't heard any of the screaming before. Maybe they didn't want to hear anything. Maybe we were sounding like we usually sound, even with that demon banging around and all that yelling. But Alice's howling brought them out of their houses, looking at the sky, looking at the trees, staring down alleys, inching up to Dumpsters and cans, looking for that sound.

Mom took Alice back into her bedroom and wouldn't let any of us in there. The demon had passed out altogether, so Dad and Tony passed the time by clipping off the demon's claws with a pair of hedge clippers. Those claws were pretty splintered up by the time they were through with them. Finally Mom came out and said Alice was only getting worse, and they should take her to the hospital. Dad carried her out and put her in the back seat, and Mom stood looking at us. We knew she had orders to give. We listened real carefully. She said, "By the time I get back I want that demon out of here. I don't care how you do it, just make sure it's gone." She drove off, real dangerous looking.

❀   ❀   ❀

I don't know where all the time went, but it was getting dark. I thought that Dad would take that demon off someplace and never tell us where, but he made us all go with him. He took his rifle with him, so Tony got his, and I was afraid for the demon's life and didn't even think the demon would survive the ride in Tony's trunk. He did, though. We took him off on an old logging road that ran through a forest, until the road was blocked off by an old fallen tree. Dad and Tony took the demon out of the trunk and tossed him down so hard—he wasn't that heavy anymore—that his head cracked against a stump. The demon was almost wasted away, and I couldn't help feeling guilty that we hadn't fed him anything, not even a last meal. But then he didn't have a mouth so how could we?

"Should we leave him all tied up?" Tony asked.

"No, loosen his ropes, son," Dad said, and then Dad pointed his gun at the demon. "Demon?" he screamed. "Hey you, demon! Damn you, get up and start running! I'll give you five seconds!"

Dad counted, but I don't know if a demon can count any better than Dad can shoot. He just sat there with his eyes closed, and at the count of five the demon hadn't moved, and Dad had blown a hunk of sod and twigs to smithereens. Then the demon's eyes came open real slow, and he tried getting up, but he was too slow at it, so Tony took a shot and narrowly missed a tree about two miles away. Their aim was awful, but they didn't want to admit it, no way. They said they were just trying to scare the demon off.

The demon looked at what was left of its splintered-up claws, real sad. He looked at me and looked sadder still and started working around his jaw again. I knew I'd let him down real bad. I could tell he felt like crying. But what could I do? Maybe all he wanted was to tell us his name, and then we might've gotten him to mind, but you can't even begin to get a demon to mind you if you don't know his name—so I worked real hard for those last few seconds. I tried to guess. He worked around his jaw, and I closed my eyes, while Tony and Dad stood there with their guns shaking in their hands. At least with a dog you can give it a name, and if you say it long enough the name might stick. But with a demon you have to guess—or you have to be told—and that demon's lips were locked together like God had given them a pinch before he kicked him down to earth. So I gave up. I looked at the demon and shrugged, and I swear I saw the demon shrugging back—as sorry and helpless as I was—before he started to climb the hill, vanishing in the dark.

"We probably got rid of it well enough," Dad kept saying to himself as we drove back, but he didn't sound very convinced about it. It took us forever to get home. We got ourselves stuck in a couple dead ends and took about a dozen wrong turns. Virgil kept whining, "We're lost!" but Dad said, "No, we're not. We're just trying to put that demon off our trail." I knew the truth, though. I felt all turned around. North was south and east was west until we finally got back to the house. Mom and Alice were already there. The folks at the hospital were real curious about the demon scratch, so Mom had lied and said a cat scratched her. As far as the miscarriage went, Alice said that was a false call. Tony looked halfway disappointed about that. But anyway Alice was looking a lot better, and I guess the demon got a lot better, too, because he covered a lot of miles to be back in our closet that morning. We must have took that demon out of the closet a dozen times. We still haven't gotten rid of him. We've tried about everything we could.

One time we drove him into the city and gave him an old jacket and a bottle of wine, and we dumped him by a Dumpster. One time we tried ditching him in a motel room. We tried ditching him in the dog pound real late one night. We tried to ditch him in a homeless shelter. In a bus shelter. In a parking lot. All tied up in a church basement. How many times is that? We've tried everything, and now with Alice's ugly baby we're more crowded than ever. Alice and Tony and their little monster sleep in Virgil's room. Virgil and Mom sleep in Mom and Dad's room. Regan claims she sleeps with Jesus but actually she sleeps alone. I sleep on the couch, because I'm not ever going to forgive her. Dad sleeps in the basement. Virgil says soon we'll have plenty of room. He says he's putting a little more gasoline in Dad's tea every day.

The demon sleeps in the closet. He's the only one with plenty of room because it's his closet now, and he doesn't need much room. One time Dad came in real excited because he thought he'd found some guy who wanted to buy the demon. That didn't work out, though, but nobody was disappointed, because nobody really cared. For a long time, I wanted to take the demon to school and show him off, but nobody would let me, and now I don't even want to anymore, because that demon doesn't say nothing or do nothing. I'd rather have a dog. At least with a dog you can give it a name and get it to sit down and speak and punish it if it starts to beg. That demon just blinks and scratches up the walls. One time we forgot about him for about a month. The only good thing you could say about a demon is that he costs almost nothing to keep, a lot less than that baby does. That baby takes the food right out of my mouth. Sometimes you don't even want to take a breath for fear that baby has had it first. And that baby's got teeth now. Sometimes that baby screams all night long.

A Bad Case of Honesty

HERE'S HOW IT all started. I met up with her at the chick hatchery, one of the lousiest jobs around, apart from the pay. We were on the line that clipped the wings, and we did this all day with band saws. I want you to imagine that for a second, standing there all day and slicing off the wing tips of those baby chicks. We're not just talking clipping feathers here. It's bloody work, but the smell was the worst of it. Anyway, she was new there. I noticed her right off. She looked back at me, too, but then about three o'clock she finally yelled at me, "What're you looking at, asshole?" and the boss overheard this. He was a proper man, you know, always claiming a higher purpose, like "serving the community," lies like that, and he said, "Georgette?"

Right off she fingered me, blaming me, which surprised me more than anything else because you don't do that at a job like this, so I had to think fast. I told the boss that I had a bet with the other guys about how long it would take for her to lose a finger. She said, "You're a damn liar," and the boss said, "Georgette?" No, sir, I said. I said we were all worried for her, because she was blinking her eyes just as she stuck the chick's wing against the band saw, and she yelled out, "That's a lie!" But then, sure enough, right after the boss walked off, she nicked herself, not that bad, not that you'd know it from how she yelled out. I said, "So I guess I'm not such a liar after all," and we all gave those little chicks a rest while we came to help her, getting her bandaged up and back to work. She didn't have but the smallest sliver of a fingertip gone, plus most of the nail, but she had the most beautiful long fingers I'd ever seen. Plenty to lose there. When I looked at those hands I was hooked.

Anyway, we started hanging out after work. Maybe that surprises you, but it shouldn't. She had a pretty low opinion of humanity in general, and I wasn't much lower, so she didn't mind me that much. The thing is, she hated being alone. It didn't take too long after that to hit on the subject of "the truth" and how she was about it. We slapped up against that wall I don't know how many times. Well, I tried to argue with her. I said that there are limits on how much truth you can tell or even want to tell, and everyone knows it. I even tried to give her a for instance. I said, "Take someone who's just lost their job." Like you're going to, I was going to say, but I didn't. I said, "You know it's their fault, but you know that if they get depressed and lose faith in themselves then they might not find another job, and so you tell them that—"

She stopped me. "You're making that up," she said.

"Of course I'm making it up. It's an example."

"You can't just make up a story to make it fit the point you're making."

"Okay then, so what's the difference between telling a lie and just being wrong?"

She knew what I was talking about. She was always making mistakes. For example, we had this big argument about the difference between a tornado watch and a tornado warning, and there were other things she was wrong about, too.

"Wrong is wrong," I said.

"Look," she said. "There are lies and then there are mistakes. You tell lies. I make mistakes, and you're one of them. You're not exactly an honest mistake, either." And she didn't even smile.

That's how it was. She never did think I was an honest person. Mostly it was because of the things I'd say to my boss to make him happy. I tried telling her that's how the world is. You lie to bosses. And as far as I could see, it was a big mistake not to. But that was a mistake she was determined to make. You see, every Easter the first graders make a tour of the hatchery, and Georgette got a bug in her ear about it, so she made the mistake of telling those kids about what those little chicks go through. She called it "the truth," but the boss called it "insubordination," and he fired her. But it worked out okay. Right off, she got a job painting houses, where her boss didn't really give a damn what she thought. It just didn't matter. It was what you call honest labor, and it suited her fine, except it was seasonal work.

I don't think she ever lied to me once, not even after she had this thing going with a man she met at the bakery. That's where she was working after she had to give up painting because her hands were getting stiff from the cold. Anyway, about that time I got really interested in the truth myself. I used to torture myself with it, asking where she'd gone, had she seen him, the first time they had sex, blow by blow. She told me everything. Of course, I knew deep down it was a mistake to learn all the details. I'd just sit around and try to imagine the truth about what they were doing, and making up excuses to torture myself, like

telling myself I had to face the truth. But sooner or later, the truth started to eat up every other thought I had, like the biggest fish in the tank.

Finally I said to her, "You know, I'm starting to think that wanting
to know the truth is one big mistake, as big a mistake as always telling
the truth. And if a mistake is something that's wrong, then the truth just
might be another kind of lie."

She stared at me like I was covered with dirt and said, "Listen. Who
knows what the truth is, but a lie is a simple thing. Just because we're
confused about what the truth is, that doesn't let us off the hook about
lying, so don't kid yourself about it."

So then I was back at it, asking for details about her and that guy. It
was stupid. It was like she gave me an excuse to keep asking these questions. I probably gave him more attention than I ever gave her. And the
worst thing was that we were still living together then. I'd come home
from the hatchery; she'd come home from the bakery. She'd wash the
flour off her hands, and I'd wash the blood off mine. On the nights she
didn't go out to be with him, we'd talk about him, going through the
whole business. Even after she moved out we'd have these conversations
in shopping lines or walking up and down the sidewalk. People used to
think we were mad at each other over this whole business, and so they'd
leave us alone, like you do when couples are fighting. But it wasn't
fighting, it just sounded that way, and when it comes down to it, it was
some of the better times of my life. But then right after she moved out
of my place something happened at the bakery, too, something involv-
ing the bug count in the wheat and some loud remarks she made at the
Christmas party, so Georgette was out of work again, and since it was
still winter, she couldn't fall back on painting.

Sometimes she'd call me up late at night. Her way of saying hello was
to ask, "What're you doing?" as if she had already caught me at something. So I'd get jittery as soon as the phone would ring and make up
excuses even when I'd just been taking a nap. Not that I was up to anything much. I mean, a guy has to move on, right? Okay, so there was
this woman at the bar named Cass, which wasn't her real name anyway.
It was the name she went by. The thing with Cass started because I was
probing her for details about Georgette and the baker, because Cass was
a barmaid and knew things. Cass would say, "Yeah, they were in here
together. She had those claws of hers in him all night long," and I'd nod
my head as if I knew what that was all about, thinking about Georgette
and those long beautiful fingers of hers, with that little bit of a fingertip
missing. I never did tell Georgette anything about Cass, not even that I
was seeing her. I was going to, but Georgette found out before I could
tell her, so then she accused me of lying and sneaking around. The other

thing I can't explain is that one night Georgette and the baker had some kind of fight, so Georgette came over to my place and slipped under the covers. It just happened. And I told Cass about it the next day, who knows the hell why. Cass screamed at me and told me I smelled. I'll always remember that. "You stink," she yelled, and I couldn't really argue with her about it since I was always walking around with the smell of burned feathers in my skin.

But I'll tell you what really bothered me. After Georgette and the baker got back together, I found out that this guy had a bird, a cockatoo. I mean, Christ, imagine that. And he let it fly around all over his house. Anyway, the main trouble with that cockatoo was that it gave me something to fix on, since it was pretty easy for me to imagine that cockatoo flying over their bed while they were, you know, screwing and all that, and the thing was, I mean the thing that almost drove me out of my mind, was that she hated birds almost as much as I did! So I sat around and I thought about that bird. I thought about them teaching that bird cute things to say, and the bird saying them right back without knowing a damn thing about what it all meant, and I thought about her and that baker having the same conversations I had with her.

You know what she told me once? She said it only takes one lie to make a life go to hell. Because you need two lies to back up the first, then you have to tell four more to make the first two make sense, and on and on, and soon your whole life is spent keeping up the lies, like a big animal that needs a lot of food and water. She said the worst thing is that the lies get so out of hand that you get confused. You can't keep them straight, and soon the only choice you have is to leave town and start over. Or maybe you can't see them. Maybe you don't even know what they are. That's the worst thing, she said.

Anyway, about then she got her job back at the hatchery. She was back on the line, clipping wings again. The boss made a big speech about how he believed in giving people second chances, but the truth was that he had a hard time finding people willing to clip chicken wings all day long. I tell you, he sure as hell didn't have any problem keeping his lies straight at all. So then it was around Easter again, which is when we always get the first graders making their yearly tour, like I said before. Every year, we'd dye a bunch of chicks pink and light green, and the little kids came in with their shoe boxes, and then after we showed them the whole operation, we'd send them home with a little chick in a box that was going to die in about a day or a week.

I knew ahead of time what Georgette was going to do. I mean, it wasn't like she'd changed or anything. And I knew she was going to get fired all over, but I just let it happen. Those kids came in, holding hands, and we showed them the incubators, and we showed them those clean, glass-sided cages, and we didn't show them the band saws and the clipping line, and she kept her mouth shut. But then, just as we were going to let those kids pick out a fluffy little chick for their own, she started to scream at us.

"Don't you people know that this is a horrible thing to do? I mean, this is just horrible! It's one thing to send these chicks off to a farm where some family needs to raise them, even if it's at the chicken's expense, but how can you send these chicks off to die in some poor kid's bedroom?"

That never got much of a response, so she said, "Hey, you kids, do you want to wake up some morning real soon and find a dead chick in a shoe box? Do you want to pick it up with your bare hands so you can bury it? And what if these chicks actually live, have you thought of that? What's going to happen then, when you come home to a full-grown chicken clucking and scratching in your bedrooms?"

Of course the chicks were cute and round and pink and green, and the first graders really wanted them, so they cried, all of them, and all at once. The boss made a face like he had something caught between his teeth, which was his way of trying to look like he was giving some real thought to what she was saying, which he wasn't. Those teachers were looking like people do when they find out that nobody, absolutely nobody likes them. And after those kids were gone—with those doomed little chicks peeping in their shoe boxes after all, by the way—Georgette got her pink slip. She wanted me to stand by her and quit, too, but I said that would just be foolishness, especially since I'd just been made foreman of the clipping line. I'll be damned if I'd let all that sucking up to the boss go to waste. She was right about the chicks, though. I told her so. But the thing is she really needed that job.

I tried to tell her that people like us can't afford to be so honest, but she told me that honesty mattered more than a lousy job like that. After that, she decided to try a hand at waitressing, but she always told the customers what she thought about the food, and when she was angry, she slammed the plates around. She didn't last three days at that one. I used to think that one of the advantages of getting ahead in the world was that you'd eventually have enough power to be honest with people. You'd think it would be like that, wouldn't you? But it's not like that at all. You see, right now I'm thinking that some people, no matter how powerful they get, just keep lying like it's a habit, even when they don't have to, when no one can touch them. Like my boss, for example. He could be the most honest man in the world if he didn't have to believe he was a good man on top of it all. And then you have some poor waitress who's fired because she's warning somebody about the pork chops. Anyway, she got a job painting houses until it got cold and her fingers got stiff again. Then that baker managed to get her her job back at the bakery. They're still together and I'm still alone, although sometimes she calls me up and tells me all about him. Things have been kind of stuck there for a while now.

Sometimes I come out of the hatchery with the smell of burned feathers in my nose, and right off I smell the burned sugar of her bakery. It's a big, industrial bakery, a bread and cookie factory. You know, I've actually been over to that baker's apartment. This is a small city. Hardly anyone is a stranger. Word gets around fast that way, too. So I could imagine his place, which was shared by a group of young men, and it had that look. They kept it straightened up, but it was not kept very clean. I really couldn't see how she could stand it. It has several fish tanks, an oversized television, and a cockatoo, like I say, that they would let fly loose. Birds make my skin creep, especially when they're affectionate, and this one would land on your shoulder and nip at your ear lobe. She told me that.

Well, anyway. That's where it stands now. It's exactly 12:27 now, just after midnight, and I know exactly what they're doing now, and I'm just writing it all down, calling it as I see it. Maybe my hands aren't as used to lying as my mouth is; maybe that's why I'm writing this. Anyway, about now, she's in his bedroom, where they are undressing each other. I've seen this man shoot pool at the bar, and so I can imagine his skinny ass as he bends over her, as he crawls on top of her. She empties her mind, closes her eyes—and when she opens them again he's staring right at her, he's grimacing, I mean it's a scary face he's making, and then he comes, loudly, probably scaring the hell out of that cockatoo. It's probably shrieking and batting its wings against the window right now, and I'm thinking, Serves that damn bird right. That bird is getting exactly what it deserves.

Saint Anthony and the Fish

THE ROAD WHERE Ned had discovered the nun connected Dunning, Nebraska, to Arnold, Nebraska. Rand McNally took it off their maps a few years back, but the road's still there, and it's still got a pretty good surface. It runs by Ned's farm and ranch and two others. There's not a reason in the world for anyone who's not from around there even to be on this road unless they're lost. The way Ned had it figured, the nun must have been driving through late at night because she was there in his driveway at eight in the morning, sleeping in the front seat. She was already sweating. Her license plate said Pennsylvania, which made no sense at all, no matter which way you were going.

"You got problems, Ma'am?"

She rolled down the window a crack and said, "I've run out of gas."

"Well, that don't sound too serious," Ned said. "But I do think your problems will be a lot worse if you stay in that car with the windows rolled up." Ned considered the fact that what he had just said perhaps sounded like a threat, so he added, "What I mean is that you might get heatstroke."

He caught a glance of himself in her window: he hadn't shaved in days—saw no need to, really, since his wife left him, and he hadn't felt much need even before.

"I'm fine," the woman said. She kept the window up, the doors locked.

He tested the weight of the gasoline can in the back of his pickup and said, "I can get you back on the road, but I'm going to have to go into town for gas. I'd siphon you off some of my own, but the last time I did that I nearly went blind, so if you don't mind I'd rather not take the chance. You can ride with me if you want. Be a damn sight cooler than sitting in that car with the windows rolled up."

"I can wait," she said. She was dressed in a heavy black dress buttoned up to her neck, with a white collar and white cuffs, all soaked through with her sweat.

"Well, I'm serious, Ma'am. If you feel like you're getting too hot, you'd better walk up to my house. Door's open. Don't take any chances, okay? At least get out into the open air, maybe sit in the shade of that tree over there." He pointed at the tree, the only tree.

"I'll be fine," she said, and rolled up the window.

In town, Ned pulled into the gas station where a large-headed chocolate Labrador named Walrus was sleeping in the shade of the pumps. Ned knew the name of every man, woman, and dog in this town. The owner of the station was on his back with his head under a car, so after Ned filled up the red gas can, he walked over and grabbed the man's ankle, causing him to thrash and bump his head. "Damn it, Ned!"

"Sam? If I were a criminal, you'd be dead. Is your cash register open?"

Sam rolled out from under the car and said, "I hope to hell you have exact change. I haven't had time to get to the bank."

"You mean to tell me you don't even have change for just a ten?"

"Just write yourself a tab, will ya? I'll bill you when it's enough to be worth my time." Sam slid back under the car.

"I've got a woman out in front of my farm who's out of gas," Ned said. "I'm helpin' her get back on the road. It's too wet to mow hay anyway. Fact is, from the look of her, I think she's a nun. I'll put a six-pack of soda pop on my tab, too, if that's okay."

Ned wrote up his tab and put that in the empty cash register. Sam hadn't been kidding. He put the six-pack in his beer cooler. The ice had turned to water overnight, but it was still cold, the beer cans resting at the bottom like bright stones in a clear pond. Before going back to his farm, he stopped by the Cattlemen's Café to pick up something for the nun to eat, experiencing a great deal of indecision about what kind of thing he should feed a nun. The waitress suggested tuna melts. By the time he got back to her car, she wasn't in it. Squinting his eyes, he scanned the horizon. She wasn't under that shade tree, either, and he didn't see any black shape hunkered over in the grass. He drove up to his house, but she wasn't anywhere about. He might have considered this whole episode a dream or such except for the car. The car was still there. So where in the hell was that nun? Finally he walked into his barn, and there she was, seeming to be asleep and lying in the hay. "Ma'am? Are you all right? You okay?"

When he tried to help her up she called out, "Oh! Lord! Oh!"

"Land sakes, I'm not goin' to hurt ya. You're gonna hurt yourself if we don't get you in the house, so don't argue."

She blinked and looked around. "I thought this *was* your house," she said.

"This is my damn barn, lady," he said, growing impatient. "I don't know where you come from or where you got the idea that we put hay in our houses, but I've got half an idea to pack you in ice as soon as we get you inside."

With his shoulder under her arm, he walked her across his farm lot. Occasionally, she started and tried to pull and twist away from him. "I'm gonna run a cold bath," he said, deciding to be tough about it. "And you're gonna get in."

"Please," she said, "no, please."

"I'll put you in, dress and all if I have to. And I've got soda pop here, too," he said. "But drink it slow or you'll get a headache."

He got the nun a soda out of the cooler and, after pausing for a second, decided he wanted a beer. The woman stared at him while he drank it. "It's maybe a bit early," he said. "I'll own up to that. But you've given me quite the scare." She had a look about her like she hadn't been outside in a year, like she could tan in the moonlight. Her skin had a faint blue, almost transparent look to it.

Ned took some steel wool into the bathroom with some dish detergent. The tub was almost gray and black, and he had to work quite a while before it was acceptable to anyone but himself. He could hear his floors creak as the woman finally got up and started moving around. When he'd finished scrubbing, he found that the woman was staring at a photograph of his ex-wife.

"I'm divorced," Ned explained. "I'm not proud of it, but that's how it is."

While she was bathing, he took the opportunity to feed his pigs and make sure they had enough water. The pigs were all waiting on one side of the pen. Their breakfast was long overdue and they knew it. They were mad at him. They nudged and pushed, nipping at his pant legs.

Ned's wife had left him for many good reasons, but none of them serious. Simply enough, Ned wasn't a very clean man. He wasn't a very smart man. His farm never made much money, but he didn't have any debts. He drank too much, but not much too much, and he wasn't mean about it. He worked hard, from sunup to sundown. Winters he didn't have much work to do, so he made work, but none of it was geared to making life any more comfortable. He mended fences and he checked on his cattle. He was a dull man, maybe. His wife really had only one friend in town, and when that friend moved away, their life together fell apart. It wasn't really that nasty a divorce. His wife moved away more to be closer to her friend than to get away from him. She still liked him and told him so whenever she wrote him, which wasn't very much. And so the main reason why his wife left him was that their hometown had little to offer, and Ned did little to add to the nothing. A few more inches of rain each year and maybe they would have had something. A little trip now and again—even to the Black Hills—might have helped, too.

At night, sometimes, Ned could feel that nothing creep right up to the house and almost stare in the windows. In the morning Ned could still feel the nothing hanging around, like the old men in the Cattlemen's Café. It didn't bother him, though. Nothing-to-do was like room temperature to him. But in a way he felt sorry that his wife had moved out before this nun had showed up. This was the kind of thing his wife always looked forward to happening, when it never did. Not that she wanted to get a visit from a nun specifically, she just wanted a change of some kind, any change, really. Ned couldn't understand this, even though he wanted to. He couldn't understand wanting a change for its own sake. It made no difference to him. It was like some strange food that he never acquired a taste for, and so he never craved it, never missed it.

For a long time after getting out of the tub and dressed again, the nun surveyed the living room, occasionally sniffing at the air. Watching her, Ned became aware of whatever she was looking at. There were Christmas cards from many years back, magazines his wife subscribed to that he hadn't cleared away, junk mail opened by his ex-wife's hand with the unopened junk mail piled on top of it. Ned saw that anyone with a detective's mind could pinpoint the month and year when his wife got fed up and left. All the clues were here.

"I don't keep a very clean house," he finally said. She smiled and continued to look around. There were mourning doves moaning in the yard, cows moaning farther away. Ned became aware of what sounds she'd hear, what smells she might smell. She walked to the window and opened the curtain, and sunlight fell into the room.

"Rained here all last week," Ned said. "Kept me out of the fields or else I'd be mowing hay right now. It's gonna make a good second cutting, though."

She grew very still as she stood in the sunlight, which was streaming with dust.

"Yes?" she said. At first Ned thought that she was talking to him, but then she again said, "Yes?" and he hadn't asked her anything. She closed her eyes and put her arms out. With her standing there in the stream of sunlight, he felt like he was watching an old home movie of someone he was supposed to know but didn't recognize anymore. With his parents dead, his wife gone, there was no one he could even ask about it.

She turned and looked at him. At that moment, he realized that she hadn't looked at him directly before. Suddenly she reached out to touch his forehead, and he stepped back from her, too shocked to do anything but smile.

❀   ❀   ❀

Ned took a load of hay out to his pasture and spread it on the ground for the cattle there. It was hot, an unusually muggy day, and the air buzzed with cicadas. Grasshoppers splashed around his legs as if they'd been riled up by the recent rains. He drove across his field and discovered a ruptured fence line, which he mended. In this field there was a huge puddle that wasn't there a week ago. There were sandpipers strutting on the shore, and there were cattle in the water up to their knees. At the end of the day, he drove back to his house, seeing her car still in the driveway. She was cleaning his kitchen. He didn't know what else to do except offer her a room for the night, although it bothered him when he heard her praying out loud, at the top of her voice. At one point, he woke up with a jolt, because he thought she was praying right over his bed.

The next morning, by the time he got up, she was already making breakfast. When he came into his house later that afternoon, the living room was full of light. She showed him an old cathedral-like radio she discovered in the basement, which turned out to work just fine, pulling in stations from far away, and she stayed another night. The next day, she showed him an old farm tool she discovered in a shed nearly lost in the cedars and underbrush of the shelterbelt. He told her it was an old-time corn planter. "It's what my grandfather used when they still planted corn by hand," he said. "I'd never bothered to plant corn about here myself because it'd just shrivel up anyway. It's too dry."

"But this tool, can it still be used?"

"Well, sure, but it's way too late to plant corn," he said.

The next day he discovered that she'd found a bag of old seed corn in the barn, and she was planting this corn right next to his house. It bothered him. He didn't like to see her work as hard as this and all for nothing. Of course as the weeks passed there was talk around town about this guest he had. Sam gave him strange looks, and whenever he walked into the Cattlemen's Café the crowd went silent, but soon enough it seemed natural that she was there. Most nights when he came home from the fields, she would be out walking about in his pasture. Her hands would be clasped behind her back as if she were thinking about something. Or she'd be out near that pond that had risen with the recent rains, staring at the water. When she'd see him, she'd wave, and start on back. After a while, she started talking to him. She started slow at first, as if she weren't that used to it, but then she started talking a lot. She told him about her order, its mission, their silences and songs. Ever since she was a child she had planned to be a nun, she said. She was frequently disappointed. Work was prayer, she said. Her greatest temptation was that she longed to be extraordinary.

Sometimes after supper, she'd show him something she'd discovered in his attic or basement or one of the extra rooms that had filled up with junk over the years. Almost every day, she found whatnots and keepsakes that she packed into the china cabinet where the china had long ago been harvested for everyday use. As the summer wore on, the hay was thick, the cattle were fat. More rain than he remembered in years, and the pond in his pasture had become the habitat for pelicans, beautiful white pelicans.

What's more, the old seed corn she had planted was starting to grow. No way would it mature, but that hardly seemed to matter. For the first time, as long as he could remember, Ned wondered what would happen next. He felt ill at ease but in a pleasurable way, as if he were letting a horse he was riding run as fast as it wanted. One night she asked him if he believed in miracles, if he knew what they were. He had to admit he'd never given it much thought. In his life, it had been more a matter of taking day by day and accepting what came. She laughed when he told her that, and then she told him the story of a man who couldn't stop preaching. Whenever people gathered around him, he preached to them. He couldn't help it. One day he traveled to a deserted shore to rest his voice, but when he saw the fish he started preaching to them, too. He couldn't help preaching, and the fish couldn't help listening, their heads poking out of the water to listen, their pink lips puckering as they concentrated on his words.

He smiled and nodded, more at the joy she took in telling the story than the story itself. In fact, he didn't really know if he understood her meaning. But that didn't mean the story had no effect on him. In fact, ever since first hearing that story, he started to wonder if there were fish in his cattle pond. The pelicans seemed to think so. They stepped lightly on the shoreline and studied the water, and every time he saw this, he thought about her story.

As the summer passed, he ordered chicks through the mail for the first time in years, and they all survived shipment. Cats wandered onto the farm and stuck around. When the fall came, the pelicans left. The pond froze over, and he was glad for that. It would keep its secrets locked up through the winter. Usually he didn't have much to do in the winter unless he had cattle and pigs. That winter he sold them off, the chickens too, so he could spend more time working on his house. When he tore out the old lead pipes, he found the wedding ring of his great-grandmother, caught in a water trap. When he moved the ancient refrigerator, he found an old closet door behind it. There was a wedding dress inside, his great-grandmother's wedding dress, and layette gowns and bonnets and booties. Without her he would not have known these words.

One day in February she began packing her car. He followed her around the house, letting her pile her few possessions into his arms, and when they were finished, she said to him, "Ned, you're a good man, but I don't think you even know what that is." She reached out and touched his cheek, and he blushed, his face continuing to feel warm in the cold as he watched her drive off. She left fresh tracks in the snow. Darkness fell. He tried to make himself a supper. He burned his eggs. He noticed that the bread had molded and the milk was rancid. He noticed that the melting snow from his boots had soiled the carpet. He was afraid that his house was returning, almost before his eyes, to the state it had been in before she arrived. Later he walked out to the frozen cattle pond where they had walked almost every night. He looked for fish frozen in the ice, their heads sticking out, their mouths open in astonishment.

He knew she was gone for good when she hadn't returned by midnight. The farm was empty. Even the cats that made their summer appearance had drifted away, and the nothing that had always been just outside his window had finally made itself at home. He stayed up late, listening to the wind, waiting for it to speak to him. He wrote a letter to his friend Sam. "All the cattle are gone, the pigs and chickens, too," he wrote. All at once he knew that he had been preparing for this moment, selling his farm off piece by piece. "I'm gonna be gone awhile, too, so look in on the house every once in a while if you can. Make sure it doesn't leak. I'd hate to see all my good work spoiled."

At the first sunlight, the snow a pale red, the sky a deep blue, he carried a bag out to his pickup and drove away, making more fresh tracks. Hers had already been covered over, since it had been snowing all night. He did not know where he was going or how he would find her. As he drove through town, he saw that there was nobody on the street. He stopped at Sam's Service Station and left his note on the door, and he noticed that the old Labrador Walrus was standing on the wide street looking at something that he couldn't see, the snow coming down, seeming to circle its giant head. Ned took this as a sign: the dog was staring down the town's only road, so he followed it. He drove forever. Small creatures came out of the fields, came right up to the road to watch him drive past. There were wild geese flying ahead of him, guiding him. There were sun dogs in the sky above him. There was a warm wind rushing out before him, brushing the new snow out of his path.

Bonehead

SHE WAS JUST outside the park, painting children's faces. When she looked up, her eyes stayed on me for a moment before she turned back to her work, her long absurd eyelashes seeming to flutter in the wind. A black outline of a smile surrounded her mouth. A black triangular nose, a Raggedy Ann dress, a carrot-color wig. I continued to stare at her. "Do I know you?" she finally asked, and as soon as I heard that voice, I said, "Sarah?" Her real mouth fell open. "Rover?" She stood up. The kid who'd been sitting on her lap slipped to the ground with a pretty hard bump. "Red Rover?"

I didn't know what to say, because it was Sarah herself right in front of me, her face coming right out of that clown's face. It was like looking into the face of a friend who had changed in some terrible way, through illness or age, and you feel like you're trying to keep your own face from showing how shocked you are. It was *her* face, hers. Her arms went around me. I could feel the tips of her floppy, oversized shoes clapping down on top of my feet. The fright wig came off and the angelic golden hair, the swirling hair that had been Sarah's trademark in the days that I knew her—oh God, that hair floated down to her shoulders. "Oh, Rover baby," she said, "You're really here?" Fat yellow tears glided down her white cheeks.

She left her children for a while, and we held hands while we walked through the park. Occasionally she scratched her head, which must have itched terribly from having to wear that horrible wig. She told me that she had to go back to work and finish up the day, but we both agreed that we would meet later that evening to catch up. I planted kisses on the red dots that covered each of those famous fat cheeks of hers, and I watched her run back to the children, lifting her feet high to keep from tripping over her toes.

❀   ❀   ❀

An old drunk was at the end of the bar, playing "Mr. Sandman" on an imaginary trombone. I'd seen his trick before—he'd purse his lips and fill his whole head up with sound, and it really did sound like a trombone. Aside from him and the bartender, no one else was there when Sarah walked in. It disturbed me to see that she was still in her clown getup. She even had that wig on. The bartender smiled when he served us, but he didn't say anything.

"Did you know," she said, "that Golden Dan's a forest ranger now? You remember how shy he was. Because he was always so beautiful. Shy and beautiful. And he likes his job. Because the fall in the forest is very beautiful. And shy. He says he feels like he's in camouflage. And Saint Anthony? Have you heard that he sells life insurance? He has such an honest face. Isn't it nice that we all have jobs that are so right for us?"

When she said that, I was silent for a while as I studied the clown makeup. There was probably a sad story behind it. For a while I thought about her dream of being an actress.

"So what are you doing now?" she asked. "Not now now, but every-day now."

"I file X rays," I said. "A through Z." The spooky thing about her clown face was that no matter what I said, she looked like she was smiling. "I don't think I'll work there much longer. A temporary position."

"Until your ship comes in?" I could hear the slapping of her floppy shoes under the table. She must have been nervous. "Just until you get your new orders, right?" The sound reminded me of Thumper in Bambi. "Just until you earn enough for your passage home? Then you'll go a-roverin', just like always?" The balloon of her smile grew large and tense.

"Is something wrong?" I asked.

Suddenly she burst out crying. The man with the imaginary trombone was playing "The September Song" all by himself. The bartender stared at us and started shuffling bottles, pretending to restock his shelves. "What's wrong, Sarah?" I slid over to her side of the booth. I put my arms around her. She had trouble finding her words.

"But you had such big dreams!" she said. "You wanted to . . . to see . . . to see . . . to see past things, inside things, things like that!"

I didn't even really know what she meant by that. It was probably something I once said to her that I couldn't remember anymore. Some wishful thinking on my part that stood out in her mind only because she had so few memories of me. A big tear slipped off her greasepaint like a small man off an icy roof.

"Hey, Sarah," I said. "I'm okay, really."

Or maybe it was herself, her own dreams, she was crying about. Poor Sarah. For all her talent, she was always running into bad luck. We used to call her Little Miss Hapless. She hated it when we called her that.

❀   ❀   ❀

Sarah was never a very sexual woman. In fact, she was just about the most innocent person I'd ever known, so when I walked her back to her sad little apartment, I never guessed that she would suddenly grab me and push her mouth against mine so hard that it made my teeth hurt. I could feel the greasepaint smearing around on my face, and then we lost our balance because I was standing on those oversized shoes. Once again, the wig slipped off, that fine angelic hair spraying out, a little damp from sweat and needing a wash, but still beautiful. The patch-printed Raggedy Ann dress slipped off, and then her striped smock and striped tights, and suddenly she was gloriously naked, as beautiful as I ever imagined.

I hopped on one foot as I pulled off my cowboy boots, and then I crawled into her thin bed where she was waiting, her clown face glowing from the streetlight outside her window. I have no real sense of time after this. Boundaries and measurements lost meaning all together. Later, I had a hard time recalling just how she touched me, just how I touched her. The only thing I really remember is that she asked me, "Rover? Did you . . . melt?" And when I said yes, she hugged me hard, as if my melting made her very happy.

In the morning, I had the opportunity to see her take off her make-up to apply a fresh coat. Not that I doubted it, but at least for one moment, after she swabbed her face with cold cream, I saw that it was really her, the Sarah I remember. She still had that beautiful skin that was so clean and clear it almost seemed transparent. And those startling green eyes—I'd forgotten them. They seemed to look right through you, past your skin and bones, seeing you for the soul you were. It sometimes made me uncomfortable. We also called her Sarah Clairvoyant, another name she did not like.

"You're still very beautiful," I finally said, but she ignored me. A new sequin jacket. A long flowing dress. Finally, a stiff collar of a can-can-like fabric that stuck out from her neck, as if her head were being served on a plate. With her hair pushed back under the red Afro, she looked like a ghastly version of Queen Elizabeth I. Still seeming distracted, she gathered up her slapstick, her horn, her paper flowers, and stuck them in a bag, heading for the door. I followed her, feeling neglected, and maybe she realized that, because she suddenly snapped to when we reached the street. I said, "I hope I can see you again."

"Oh, Rover, Red Rover. You can always come over."

"Tonight?"

"Tonight would be fine," she said. But she walked away without say-ing good-bye. No time set, no place to meet. I could see that, from the look on her face, she was already someplace else.

❀   ❀   ❀

At work, I already had a big stack of X rays that needed filing. Black bones. Crania, femurs, metatarsals. I still had to mumble the alphabet to get them in the right slot, which always made me feel like I was about six years old. The hours crawled until my shift was over. I burst out of the hospital, squinting my eyes, so used to looking at X rays that I imag-ined I could see the bones in everything. I examined my fork and knife in a greasy spoon restaurant as I dreamed about Sarah's bones. What I mean about her skin seeming transparent is that it shows through to the faint blue undertones. But it was hard imagining her bones. I think I still imagined her being solid through and through, like a chocolate rabbit.

My life with Sarah had turned onto a dark road about seven years before. She was married when I met her, but she was leaving the man. It was already settled. Or so she said. She said that her husband dressed in drag and walked the streets of Albany. That turned out not to be true. Hardly anything she said was true, and there was much that she with-held besides. After she left her husband, I slept on her couch for weeks, supposedly to guard her from this brutal transvestite. I finally met him when he cornered me at a Halloween party, grabbing my hand with both of his and looking at me with moist, sincere eyes. He was the only one there who wasn't in costume. I was in a dog suit. Sarah was dressed as Glenda, the Good Witch of the North. He said, "I love her. Protect her." As he approached me, I was ready for a fight, so I was shocked at how friendly but haggard he looked, as if he'd been up for days.

During the whole time of our romance, I never slept with her once. Although I longed for it, I never once felt her skin against mine, so I went a little nuts when she confessed to me that she'd made love to Saint Anthony, because—she said—he reminded her of the pictures of Jesus she used to see in her grandmother's house, the ones where Jesus is knocking at the door. Maybe that was true, and maybe it was just an excuse. In either case, about two months later, Sarah disappeared for a weekend, and when she came back there were great chunks of her hair cut off. Blunt and jagged cuts—a horrible amputation. "I hate him," she said. It took me a while to figure out what happened. "I was glad to get rid of it," she said. At first, I thought she meant her hair. "I have no guilt at all," she said. On her arms and ankles, I saw the black scabs of cigarette burns. "Like stigmata," said Saint Anthony, but to me they appeared more like bug bites. She scratched at them and kept them raw.

What happened next is what shames me the most. After this, I grilled her. I interrogated her every night about why she would sleep with Saint Anthony but not with me. She said to me, "I was saving you for God!" Now who in their right mind would have believed this? So I kept grilling her. I wanted to stop the questions, but I couldn't stop them. I kept probing for her real motives, assuming that everything she said was a lie until one night, as I was asking the same questions over and over, she told me that a black angel had just come into her room. She listened carefully, and then reported that it demanded more payment then and there. She locked herself in the bathroom, but I broke through the door, flushing away all the pills I could find. And then we stopped seeing each other altogether—except for one day when we took a walk through the cemetery. A last date.

Tonight, in my current frame of mind, I still see the bones crisscrossing beneath the ground—a fall day, the leaves letting go. The acid reds of the maple trees did something to my vision. She seemed to be floating. Her jagged hair stuck out in all directions, the polished tombstones shining. And I was floating too, trying to hang on to her hand. A rolling landscape, trees and tombstones tilted. We were beyond words. Something passed between us, but then we went our own ways. I never really understood what exactly happened. It's one of the many things I've never understood, including who she was and what attracted me to her, but this is the kind of thing I think about as I'm alphabetizing clavicles and filing ulnas.

❀   ❀   ❀

The knocking woke me up. After pulling on my pants, a little confused, left leg in the right before I got it straight, I opened the five latches and there she was. A different face than she wore this morning, and only her bone structure made her face recognizable, catlike. Her smile turned down. She had X's on her eyes. "Come," she said, putting out her hand.

She took me to a neighborhood I'd never seen before, an area of warehouses by an old abandoned railroad track. She did a tightrope walk on the rails, a damaged umbrella in one hand. Nearby, a little gray light leaked out of the filthy windows of an old building. Taking my hand again she led me inside, where she produced a candle, and we crept across the broken glass. I could hear the muttering of pigeons, the occasional clapping of startled wings. A huge, dark cavity surrounded us, breathing in its space. There were chairs around a small, soiled bed. She lit a circle of candles, reaching out for me. I stared into those X's on her eyes all the time she peeled off my clothes. I don't even remember her taking off her own costume, but there we were, rocking, cradling each other while the candles guttered and throbbed. I must have fallen asleep at some point, because when I woke up, there was a circle of white faces glowing around me. I was still naked. They gathered around me, touching me everywhere, and I was moving far out of myself. Someone pulled a white robe over my head, and someone else painted me, not bothering with whiteface, just a red circle around one eye and a few black tears dribbling out of the other. One clown put a hand into the cleft of my buttocks, and I twisted and looked at who it was—an old woman, with stars on her eyes and a doglike nose. She withdrew her hand quickly and made her eyes wide, her mouth round.

Sarah's face was the same as before, two X's on her eyes like the dead men in cartoons. But her outfit was different. All white pantaloons, white pointed shoes, and a white jacket with wide shoulders. Instead of the usual red fright wig, she wore a white rubber skullcap, with a little thimble of a white hat on top.

I don't know how I could even attempt to make love to her in the presence of all these clowns. But that's what they expected of me. The old woman pulled off Sarah's pantaloons and parted her jacket. Her nipples were painted black, with white petals around them. Black-eyed Susans. I still didn't move, so the woman walked over and lifted my robe. "He's shy!" she proclaimed, and all the clowns snickered. "Come here," Sarah said. I slipped out of my robe, my flesh hanging loose and pale. We started to pump like a huge pink heart while the clowns looked on, but very soon I lost my self-consciousness. I didn't mind their rude comments. "Melt," Sarah said. And I was about to, when one clown poured hot wax on my back. I screamed as they tore me away from her, tossing me in a water tank. Every time I tried to come up for air, they pushed me back under, and the next thing I knew, I was back on the soiled mattress, one thin candle glowing. No one else was there except for Sarah. Again, I was naked. She was naked, too, but this time she didn't have any makeup on. She looked exactly like the Sarah I knew years ago—her wide face flat as a cat's, her green eyes intense and supernatural, her golden hair coiled. I reached out and touched the scars on her wrists, fresh scars seeming to cover ancient ones, a series of suicide scars. She flinched and said, "Don't—"

"I'm sorry."

"I don't want you to touch me—"

"I'm sorry."

She took my hand and put it between her thighs, a moist and secret place. She moved it, lightly. "Let us pray. . . . Red Rover, Red Rover. Send Jesus right over."

"Sarah?—"

"Don't you think that masturbation is just like prayer? Don't you feel embarrassed when you pray, as if someone walked in on you and caught you masturbating? Doesn't prayer feel nice?"

One of the clowns stepped into the candlelight for a second. He was dressed in academic robes. His green hair sprouted out from under an immense mortar cap, with a tassel that danced in his face. I became aware that there were other clowns, too, out there in the dark, watching us. I could hear them breathing. But I didn't care. She didn't have makeup on, so I wanted to stare at her face. It was my first chance to examine it, to see what she really looked like, her soft skin a blue transparency. Suddenly her face changed. A human mask. She shoved my hand away. Her face was almost terrifying. She struck herself in the head with her fist. "Don't you see?" she asked, almost pleading.

I just stared at her. I've never seen anyone so beautiful.

With a deep sigh, she gave me greasepaints and lay on her back. At first, I didn't know what to paint. So I just painted bright orange stars on Sarah's eyes—and those black-nippled, black-eyed Susans on her breasts. The clowns breathed deeply, occasionally chuckling, watching us from the outer dark.

❀   ❀   ❀

When I woke up again, the clowns were standing around me. Sarah was still naked, but now her body was covered in white, with black bones painted on her arms and legs. Her head was shaved. I found that very disturbing. A broad-faced skull enveloped the white hollow of her eyes. Someone shoved one of the clowns, and he stumbled forward, almost falling. He looked lost. He looked like someone who'd been terrorized, tortured. "This is Dolt, poor man," Sarah said. "He lost his brains on the highway. Motorcycle accident. No helmet. He tried to eat his brains, so they wouldn't go to waste, but it only made him stupider. Over here, sweetie!"

The man waddled around the room with his hand out, looking for someone to shake it. I noticed the artful cranial stitching. I couldn't tell if it was real or painted. "Poor Dolt," Sarah said, and all the clowns made mournful tisking while they struck at him with slapsticks. "But look how clever he is at getting attention," she said. "And over there is Footit, remember him?"

Another clown opened his academic robes to reveal an owl's face where his genitals should be. "Bonehead!" he said. "Look at me,

Bonehead!" And the air shivered with the clowns' plastic laugher.

"I told them about your day job," Sarah whispered. "And look, here's Lulu!"

The old woman that had so rudely handled me stepped forward. I put out my hand to shake, and she put out hers, grabbing my crotch. I stared at her, startled, and I saw past the mask. "Oh my God," I said, "you look like—"

"Like what? Like Hell? Like France?"

"Like someone I know!"

I looked around. I knew them all.

With a light squeeze, Lulu released me. In the old days, we called her Lady Mac as she scrubbed and scrubbed and scrubbed her hands. She smiled, toothless, and scratched herself. Her hand, almost on its own, went to her head and began twisting a single strand of gray and red hair. And there behind her was Scaramuccia, whom because of his shy nature we called Golden Dan, and the one Sarah called Raggedy Andy, whom we called Saint Anthony.

"What is more innocent than a child's toy," Sarah said of him, pinching his ass.

And there was Footit, whom I never got to know that well, whose cheerful disposition had always annoyed me. I even recognized Dolt, who was our pet, our idiot savant, our misfit genius.

"And surely you know my ex-husband, the fierce Grimaldi?" I looked at Grimaldi and he glared back, tearing open his shirt to show that he was wearing a bra.

"But . . . these clown suits," I said. I wanted to say something else, a question to articulate the depths of my confusion, my longing, but I didn't know what else to say, only managing a feeble "Why?"

"God wants no less than we do," she said. "God wants to be naked, but you would not be able to stand that, would you, so God puts on clothing, and we do, too."

They all gathered around me. I was truly scared about what would happen next, and with good reason. Without a word, they were upon me. I struggled. I scratched and bit as they pulled me to my back and Lulu and Grimaldi forced ridiculous bloomers over my legs and up to my crotch. Scaramuccia held a mirror to my face while Sarah knelt on my shoulders, painting bones on me and singing the alphabet song. Finishing their work, they put me into motley. Raggedy Andy took special joy in putting the coxcomb of the cuckold on my head, each horn tipped by a soft tinkling bell. But this done, they took no more notice of me.

Grimaldi began to torment Poor Dolt again, slapping him in the head and then sneaking behind him so Poor Dolt started spinning in one place, unable to tell where Grimaldi was. Lulu hiked up her skirt and unveiled her buttocks, wagging it for Raggedy Andy. Meanwhile, Scaramuccia admired himself in his mirror, not knowing that Sarah was on the other side. He admired his face in hers, and she admired hers in his, and I was even starting to have a great deal of fun when Sarah shouted out "Hush!" The clowns went silent.

"I am called by many names!" Sarah shouted as Grimaldi played a drawn-out drum roll. "And most I did not choose! Sarah Clairvoyant! Poor Sarah! Little Miss Hapless! But now I call myself by the name the clowns call me, the FABULOUS, the INCREDIBLE, the AMAZING ZANY!" A cymbal crashed. Sarah presented herself to us, arms out, turning around, her naked skin shining with the grease-black bones. She danced a bone-dance for us and played a slide trombone with considerable skill while the clowns formed a line in front of her, linking arms, shouting in unison:

"Red Rover, Red Rover! Send Bonehead right over!"

And I charged, aiming for the weakest link. Even though I understood none of this, I aimed right for Dolt, bowling him over and breaking through the line, and I almost stumbled, but she caught me, pulling me against the bones that covered her skin. When I found my feet, I looked around at the clowns who cheered and approved, tripping and falling, playing with mirrors, beating each other over the head. *What's happened? What's changed?* I turned to her, seeing the bones in her hands, the ribs underneath her breasts, the teeth behind her lips. "Who are you?" I asked. "Who are you?" she asked, and I threw my arms around her, my hands pressed against her spinal cord, still grasping for that dark twisted rope.

Land of the Midnight Blonde

LAST SUMMER, during a fierce downpour, we stood at the door of Ralph's and watched Kirby's neon start to flash and smoke. At either bar, the middle-aged and old are just a vocal minority. Mostly you see fresh faces floating through the smoke: they come of age for a year, and then they graduate, and most leave Fargo. In the fall the bar fills up with strangers who turned twenty-one in the summer months. In six months they try to look as if they've seen it all, and maybe they have. Year by year now, I watch them surface in this crowd like waves on a lake, always the same and always fascinating.

She was a new face, with honest mouse-blonde hair. I imagined that she usually hung out with boys who kept their heads under car hoods. All night they revved their engines, keeping the neighbors up. A lot of the time they ignored her, like tonight. They were out with each other tonight, and so she sneaked in the bar, obviously underage, and stationed herself right in front of me and danced. She kept glancing at me, over her shoulder, so I had to smile. She probably didn't realize how old I was. Couldn't count the rings around my eyes in the dark.

And now, another weekend, she comes up to me, this time with a name, "Shelly." She seems to know everything—that I teach classes, that I used to have a fierce and loyal girlfriend. "So why?—" she says. A pause. "Why were you staring at me the other night?" It's too honest of a question, and she asks it without a trace of inflection.

"I thought you were staring at me," I say. I have a tendency to lecture, but otherwise I have a hard time holding up my end of a conversation. I answer questions with questions. She lowers her head, looks right through me, and does not blink.

"Something definitely happened," she says—and she opens her hand, an indecipherable gesture. All these thoughts in her head, and hardly a smile to hide them with, too blank, too real. I have to look away. The band is coming on stage anyway.

They call themselves Farm Accident, and they sing ironic folk songs about random tragedy with a sense of the mythos in this place, locusts and divorce, farms that fail, lovers that toss themselves down into a well. Shelly led me into a kind of clog dance, lots of elbows and skipping in place. She smiles at me, so incredibly young and smart that I'm caught between worlds. Half my face in shadow, half my body cut off by the frame. But this is my home. I live here. I live in a state where the rivers run north.

❀   ❀   ❀

Thomas McGrath lived here, too, in the clapboard house that became the abortion clinic. Louise Erdrich also lived here, before she put the neon sign of the Pussy Cat Lounge in print. She lived in Robert's Place, an apartment with a skylight but no windows, except one, which looks into an adjoining apartment. Joel lives there now, trying to make peace with his demons, or at least to be on speaking terms with them. He's writing a book called "Pornopolis." An old girlfriend, who moved into Robert's Place after she moved out of mine, still gets Erdrich's junk mail: mass-mail coupons and funeral plans. We treasure these connections. A town needs its writers.

Wherever I see the sign in Moorhead that says Prairie Home Cemetery, I think of Garrison Keillor passing through this town. We like him, but he makes it harder for the rest of us. He's like a big wet wind blowing across the plains, and all the folksy metaphors bloom for one day and die. But when James Wright passed through, he left more behind than he took. He stood on the bridge of the Red River of the North, the hyphen between Fargo-Moorhead, and he stared down into its dark water, an emblem of death and slipping away. He found a restful place in the abandoned railroad station, hunching up beside the living tracks. Even now, the track dissects the town with crossbars and pulsing red lights, and sometimes a hobo goes beneath the wheels. Sometimes the trains jump the tracks and pile up, with heaps of coal and folded cars. But even so, it's safer to live here now than it ever was.

After arming us for Armageddon, the government has now ordered the launch codes scrambled, the silos bolted down. GIs still get isolation pay, but middle-class Norwegians send their children to finish their schooling here, which they imagine is a drug-free colony of Scandinavia, settled and homogenized by Swedes and Norwegians and Danes—and Germans too, but only the ones with the good sense to forget who they are. These children gather in Ralph's and Kirby's, foolishly drunk, singing their national drinking songs, and they are indistinguishable, except for their heavy tongues, from the general populace. As Dylan said, it's blonde on blonde—an extension of the Minnesota that made Bob Zimmerman feel like an alien. North Dakota is an extension of Minnesota in the same way that a big parking lot is an extension of a convention complex. The population peaked in 1933, and the whole state has fewer people than Omaha or Des Moines. We're definitely overrepresented in the Senate. If we possessed half a sense of honor, we'd give one senator to D.C. or Puerto Rico.

⚜   ⚜   ⚜

Let's skip a few weeks, the suicidal ones of December and January, when the temperature is a bottomless pit. Believe me, I'm doing you a favor. I tell the students in my film class that if the whole country had a similar ethnic composition, Viking movies—not westerns—would be the national film genre. Some students laugh, but Shelly doesn't. "Shelly." I leave that name and come back to that name. Sometimes I see her as the Mary Shelley portrayed by Elsa Lanchester in The Bride of Frankenstein. Lanchester also doubled as the monster's wife. I can see Shelly writing the diary of an obsessed sea captain, a man who's going farther north than anyone ever has before. She sees a scientist chasing a monster over the ice floes. She feels loyal to the scientist, more loyal to the monster. After our conversation in the bar, she decided to take a class from me— so now I see her among the other cherub faces, but serious almost to the point of lacking expression. How do you read a face so blank? Her eyes say, "I know about every lie you've ever told." Or they say: "I love you. I don't care what happens." And last night after we watched Persona, she handed me a note: "Who is the narrator of this story? Who is the I?" And then after a space: "What persona does silence project?" Whenever I see her in Ralph's or Kirby's, I try to joke with her. Nothing. Silence. She stares at me. And there's nothing more awful than the silence after a joke. It's worse than the silence after gunfire. It's worse than the silence after the scattering of crows.

But she has a friend who comes to class with her, and her friend laughs at all my jokes. I half consider enlisting the friend as my ally. Between the two of us, we might jiggle loose a laugh. My Persona lecture should be the perfect opportunity, but as I walk into the classroom, I notice—for the first time even though it's late in the term—that Shelly's friend is hugely pregnant. This puts me off my stride. I lose confidence. I retreat to plot summary:

"Persona. The Nordic temperament of this film should be familiar to you all, even if the structure is not." Nothing. Silence. "The story in itself is relatively simple. The wonderful Swedish actress Liv Ullmann plays an actress, a woman who recoils from all the personas and masks of her life—especially the mask of motherhood—by deciding to say nothing, because to say anything is a lie." Silence. "Bibi Andersson plays Alma, which means soul or psyche. She's a nurse—her role is to help her patient heal, but since the Ullmann character, Elizabeth, will not say anything, Alma rambles on—much like someone in psychoanalysis, much like—"

I was going to say teachers, but that's too close to the truth.

"Anyway, Alma begins to reveal more than she intended." I pause again. My class is even more silent than usual. Maybe the long winter is finally getting to them. Shelly watches me. Nothing is lost on her. "Partly," I say, "Bergman got the idea for the film because he thought these two blondes looked alike—and this led him to the idea of one adopting the role of the other and the violent transference, bordering on soul theft, at the heart of the film. This happens in stages. First, Andersson admires Ullmann—which develops into infatuation or puppy love: she wants to be like her. Then, like a betrayed lover, Andersson grows angry and loses herself, seeing Ullmann's silence as an aggressive denial of her human worth. She hates Ullmann, and the film, unable to contain the emotion, jams in the frame and breaks in two."

Silence. And the cowards are not even defiant about it. They stare at their desks, thinking that if they don't look at me, I won't see them.

I check my notes. "Two," I say. "Two. And one. And one and two. Notice the splitting and merging, the faces divided by shadow, divided by the edge of the frame. Notice how they start to dress alike. Light, dark, lights on and off. Anyone who's a little bipolar should understand this."

The pregnant woman giggles, although I really didn't intend that to be funny.

"I think it was John Simon who said that this film is a meditation on two and one. One breaks into two. Two merges into one. In communicating this, Bergman ironically suppresses the shot-reverse shot, the traditional method of filming dialogue. In a film with hardly more than two actresses, this is nothing less than astounding. But it's in this manner that Bergman can isolate the characters, and thus control our sense of them merging and splitting. Notice the staging and blocking, how the head of Alma moves in front of Elizabeth's head. Notice how Elizabeth is always behind Alma. And then, when Bergman finally uses the shot-reverse shot, a shot so commonplace and invisible in Hollywood cinema that it takes on the force of ideology—" I briefly think about explaining myself. "When Bergman finally uses this shot, he reinvests it with meaning. This is precisely at the point that the two faces merge into one, the ugly mask of pain and sorrow."

My class is abstracted. I can't tell what they're thinking, so I bring the lecture down to earth.

"And yet, for all the artifice and experiment in the film, there's something very ordinary about Alma and Elizabeth's relationship. . . ." I sit on top of my desk and cross my legs. "Have you ever been infatuated with someone to the point that you studied every gesture?" This gets a smile from some of them, so I'm encouraged. "And you know how it is? You really start to study them, and then sometimes you find yourself making a motion with your hands or standing in such and such a way and you think, 'Oh my God, this is just like so-and-so does it!'"

The pregnant woman laughs and gives Shelly the elbow. Shelly looks at her, annoyed and then horrified as the pregnant woman cups her hand and taps her fingers on her forehead, and Shelly turns angry and grabs the woman's wrist. The woman slouches in her seat and laughs. This little drama is over in a second, but it's a bit of a shock all the same. Because I can recognize very well that this tapping-the-forehead gesture is one of my own. I lose track of my thoughts and stare at the two women, and for once Shelly doesn't stare back.

I can't believe it: they've been imitating me, one because of infatuation, the other out of sheer mockery. What do I make of this? Old girlfriends used to imitate me, too, the way I stroked an imaginary beard, the way I held my nose when I talked. But I never knew what they were talking about until I saw myself on a Christmas videotape, just this last year, a horrifying display of gestures—some indicating an intensity of concentration and some merely goofy. The holding of my nose was the worst—I've tried to root it out of my repertory. But after thinking about it, I decided that the others really weren't so bad. A little stiff, maybe, but I didn't really think they were that noticeable.

When class is almost over, I ask my students if they have any questions. They don't want to encourage me—they don't want to stay longer than they have to—so they say nothing.

All of a sudden I say, "You don't like me, do you?"

They laugh; with a wave, I dismiss them, and Shelly leaves without looking at me, as if a line's been crossed—or crossed out. I feel sorry for her, being exposed like that, so I give the pregnant woman an evil look as she walks by, and, again, she laughs.

❋   ❋   ❋

About two weeks ago, a student came up to me and apologized for not being in class. "We had a tragedy in our family," he said, and almost calmly he explained how his young brother-in-law lost both his arms in a farm accident. He was almost cheerful. "But they've been reattached, and the doctor thinks he's going to be okay!" The next day, I see the same story in the newspaper. An eighteen-year-old falls off a grain truck, has his arms ripped off by a power take-off. He manages to run the hundred yards to his house, opens the door with his mouth, finds a pencil to punch the numbers on the touch tone for help, and sits in the bathtub, so he won't get blood over everything, waiting for the paramedics to arrive. Over the next few days, I see the story every place, even USA Today, and even my friends in Milwaukee and New York all know the John Thompson story.

I've had my own close calls with PTOs, the power take-off drives of farm equipment. They rotate at a thousand rpm. They can catch a cuff and twist you in a knot. Among the thousand ways to die on a farm, PTOs assume a fearful primacy. Around here, folks can imagine perfectly what happened to this boy, the physics of it at least, and maybe a dull version of the terror. We know what it means that the arms were ripped off, not cut off. I tell you, this accident will intrude into our dreams long after the country has forgotten it and moved on to another amazing story.

You see, there's a deeper mythos at work here, and the band Farm Accident knows this. They know that irony splits us in two, and cynicism destroys the kinder half. Despite their name, they are not cynical at all. They understand what it's like for the young people here, who leave their small towns on a heavy-metal promise. They understand the tension between the John Thompson story and an Appalachian folk song, between the public bathos and spectacle and the private tragedy. They might tease, but they like us, and they're playing at Kirby's tonight.

A slightly drunk young blonde woman comes up to me and asks me to forgive her, because every time she talks to me, she's drunk. I forgive her. A blond man grabs my shoulder and engages me in the endless handshake. He knows I teach. His name is Blaine, and I'd better remember it. Every time I look at the table where Shelly sits with friends, she looks at me, but tonight she will not come by and talk. She feels exposed tonight. A line's been crossed. But Doc will always talk to me. She's been a nanny in New York over the summer, an almost archetypal experience for the young women of my homeland. The rich of Long Island are comforted by our blonde looks, our sense of family, our confirmation lessons. Our nannies will read to their children and never lose their tempers. Our nannies are our biggest export. Another honest mouse-blonde, Doc offers me a one-hit, her spectacles slipping down her nose, so I go out and smoke by the Dumpster, hearing bluegrass music through the walls. . . .

Lovers two did jump and fall, farmer shoots his wife and dog,
People getting killed for no reason at all—folk song.

I hurry back into the bar to watch this bluegrass garage band, this augmented Peter, Paul, and Mary of the family farm apocalypse. Shelly's clog dancing on the floor, occasionally glancing at me. Doc sees a whole table waving her over. She smiles, pushing up her glasses. The crowd moves around her. Her feet go up in the air. I see Jean, not-a-blonde, but vanishing and reappearing among them even so. I'm dope-shy, so I don't talk to her, but I keep glancing at her, hoping for a smile.

Suddenly, the bar fills up with bleached blondes, pretenders who will dance to anything. They sweep through the crowd like misogyny or blonde jokes or the flu, and for a moment I feel that I will implode from self-consciousness. How foolish I must look, a middle-aged cockroach holding up a column of smoke. I grow older, but every year they stay the same age. My God, I'm too old to run with these kids.

I look up at the stage, and something strange is happening to the band. They're still singing, but I can't hear them. I look around at the crowd and they're quiet, too, as if I'm watching them at a distance with a telephoto lens. Rack focus and dissolve. Farm Accident dissolves and in their place I see the Stanley Brothers, a 1930s bluegrass band, transported from the time before the music had been tamed, and they're howling at me—

Polly, pretty Polly, your guess is about right!
Polly, pretty Polly, your guess is about right!
I dug on your grave the better part of last night!

It's a dark well I fall into, the nasal wailing of an Ozark dirge, the bitter violence of unrequited love, the loss and longing. Thank God, Barbara Cohen is there to grab me by the collar and pull me back into the bar. I hear her voice, like two strong arms reaching out to me, giving me a shake, a lift, and when I open my eyes, I see her up on the stage, the bluegrass demons gone. Skinny and sincere, she's resolutely herself when she sings, a woman of sorrows, and she's all there—baggy dress and work shoes, baseball cap pulled low over her eyes, hands on her hips, folding her elbows back so that she stands flat-footed as she sings—so I decide that I should be here, too. I live here, I like the music, and who cares what anyone thinks.

The upright bass kicks up a quick highway rhythm. Barbara Cohen whips off her baseball cap and pulls her hair into a tribal knot at the top of her head and bounces on the stage. The dance floor crowds up and over. I see Lisa, a long dress, a body shirt, a stud in her nose; and Joel in his beret, the paramilitary of the voices in his head; and Marnie, who looks like an old girlfriend; and Petra, who looks like an old girlfriend; and Kathy, who was an old girlfriend. They all push their way into the crowd and bob and sway and churn up old memories—while Shad, Marnie's boyfriend, looks on, his bad leg propped up on a folding chair: too young, too fearless, too many rodeos. Too shy to dance, Jean parodies the other dancers: she's sad, not-sad, she's Jean, not-a-blonde. And Shelly's there, too, a Frankenstein monster of blonde boy in tow. She locates me and then looks at her feet and loses herself in the rhythm, low clouds, tornadoes, freight trains in the sky. The music drives them mad. And, God, I feel good. Like Farm Accident, I'm in the spotlight, enjoying none of the crowd's appreciation, but I'm a performer too, and so I start to plan my next lecture on *Persona*.

"I have one role I play in the classroom," I'll say, "and God help me if I take it with me when I leave. But you can be sure that none of my friends let me talk as much as you folks do." Some students laugh. "You know, I like the way Ullmann pops up from the bottom of the frame and takes a picture of us. This film holds photographs of every film class who ever studied it." Some students laugh. Tomorrow, in the sunlight, the wholesome blondes will be wearing pink, the troubled blondes will be dressed in black. "If you think about acting, then you're caught between what's real and what's a mask. Writing does the same thing to you, and so does film. So think, instead, about music. There's nothing real about it, is there? Tones and scales—it doesn't sound like anything in the world. It doesn't even try. But look at what it does to you. Look at what it does to Elizabeth, when Mozart plays and shadows fall across her face. As the psychiatrist says, reality is diabolical. It'll be there soon enough, waiting for you, just like the self-immolating Buddhist monk that Elizabeth sees. Just like the photograph of the Nazi roundup. There are people out there who say it's all an act, a set of codes and signs and all a game—but look at how serious they are about it. So let them be serious. I love the way the serious people look. They're so beautiful, their faces so smooth. But don't let them stop you from going out to play. Play while you can, damn it. Class dismissed. . . ."

❊   ❊   ❊

The crowd spills into the snow-covered streets, the icy north with a mouth full of teeth. A mild Dakota winter evening, temperature in the teens. Some of the kids don't even bother with coats. I stand outside, looking around, when suddenly, Jean grabs my arm, but the crowd sweeps her away, a disappointment. I wanted to play. I look up and down the street. I feel something shift. Shelly is no one. Jean is everyone. She smiled at me before she left the bar. Maybe I'll just stand here and hang on to that smile. When the winter's gone, she'll be gone forever.

Can this be it? Can the night be over? Then I see Ron Altenburg. One night we figured out that we have the same middle name, too. R. D. A. and R. D. B., so sometimes I call him, "Ron Alter-ego." Yes, he knows about a party, so we play two Ronnies in a buddy movie, driving off into the Dakota night. We take the slow streets while he tells me that his Valkyrian girlfriend now teaches in Milwaukee. She's afraid of the night, but she's adapting: her eyes are used now to the multitude of races, so unusual here, so normal elsewhere. So when she comes home to Fargo, it seems fantastic and very unreal, like an Ice Palace full of invisible blondes.

For a while, the party is bad news, a Yugoslavia in the making. Blondes gather in the kitchen, arguing about the Kennedy assassination, arguing about abortion. I give them room. A redhead shows up, the jaundice of a bruise at the corner of her eye. A conspicuous black man shows up, and everyone wants to be his friend. Farm Accident shows up. Yes, they show up, the mythmakers themselves! And they're very nice in person. Everyone wants to feed the myth, contribute to the larger version, so we tell them about the Meckenock kid who killed his whole family, picked up his girlfriend from school, and now they're on the run like Charlie Starkweather and Ann Fulgate, like a suicide contract, a brutal folk song. We talk about John Thompson and PTOs, and I suddenly realize the point of the story. It's a story that asks you: How much do you want to live? We talk about the day-job bands, great bands that folded, gave up, got lost. That's so damn sad, to spend all that time together, all that great music, but you still end up thinking that all those years were lost. The redhead lives next door. She says, "Well, I think I'll go change," and I laugh because I think she'll come back as a blonde, because I live in a land where blonde is like protective coloration. I tell her that, and she laughs, too. It's a great party—although there are times when I open my mouth and it seems like I'm speaking in paragraphs. People nod their heads, but their eyes glass over. I'll have to watch that from now on. Leave that in the classroom. Leave that in my head.

The best part of the night is when I walk home at five o'clock in the morning. I really start to appreciate the moist wind, the fog in the air, the Nordic trees, shaggy with hoarfrost. Only for a second do I think dark thoughts. I think about Bibi Andersson grabbing Liv Ullmann's face, pinching the skin of her face, as if she were going to tear it off like a mask. It must have hurt something terrible, but the weird thing is that Liv Ullmann holds her cheek for a second and smiles. That's all. I don't know why she smiles. She doesn't say a word, and I shuffle across a frozen pond in the park, where a face seems to look up at me from under the dark ice. I don't know if it's a reflection. I don't know if it's an illusion. I just take small steps and try not to slip.

About the Author

Ron Block was born in Gothenburg, Nebraska, a town of 3,500 that currently lists thirty-four entries for Block in its phone directory. After graduating from the University of Nebraska, he moved to Kennebunkport, Maine, where he lived in a barn, and then to New Orleans, where he waited tables in the French Quarter. He attended graduate school in Syracuse, New York, receiving an M.S. in telecommunications/film and an M.A. in the Creative Writing Program of Syracuse University, studying under the poets Hayden Carruth, Philip Booth, and Tess Gallagher.

After living briefly in Minneapolis, he moved in 1984 to Fargo, North Dakota, where he taught English and film studies at North Dakota State University. In 1988 he was a winner in the Minnesota Voices competition for his book *Dismal River: A Narrative Poem*, published by New Rivers Press in 1990. In 1992 he met Jean Heinan, and within months they married and moved to Milwaukee, where he taught creative writing and literature at Marquette University and additional classes at Milwaukee Area Technical College. His son Joe was born in 1993.

Among his jobs aside from teaching, he has constructed a rodeo, bound books, written film reviews, tooled leather, and farmed with his father. More recently, he worked as a researcher and writer for a management consulting firm. Currently, he works at Mid-Plains Community College in North Platte, Nebraska, just thirty-six miles from his ancestral home. Among his duties there, he teaches English over an interactive television network to remote locations in western Nebraska. Block's poetry and stories have appeared in numerous magazines, such as *Short Story*, *The Iowa Review*, *Epoch*, *Prairie Schooner*, *North Dakota Quarterly*, *New Letters*, *Tamaqua*, and *Ploughshares*. His work has also appeared in many anthologies such as *Strong Measures: Contemporary Poetry in Traditional Forms* (Harper and Row, 1986) and *Beyond Borders* (New Rivers Press, 1992).